Mystery of the Fat Cat

The Oak Street Boys

Mystery
of the Fat Cat

by Frank Bonham

illustrated by Alvin Smith

A YEARLING BOOK

To my son, David

Published by
DELL PUBLISHING CO., INC.
1 Dag Hammarskjold Plaza
New York, N.Y. 10017

ISBN: 0-440-46226-6

Reprinted by arrangement with
E. P. Dutton & Co., Inc., New York.
Printed in the United States of America
Ninth Dell Printing—June 1979

Contents

Illustrations

1
Bad Friday

Five days a week, after school, Buddy Williams sat on a high stool at the shallow end of the Boys Club swimming pool and warned kids not to run on the wet cement. Though he was the lifeguard, he had never gotten to save anyone, because the small pool was always so crowded that it would have been impossible for anyone to sink.

Sitting up there on his stool, Buddy looked lean and graceful in his black trunks. He had a quiet brown face and faraway eyes. Buddy was a big, slow-moving boy who talked so fast he sometimes stammered. With his long arms and legs, he looked as though he could put the shot sixty feet, run ten miles, and hit a baseball out of the park.

Actually, he was not much good at anything but swimming. But when his body entered the water, like a stranded fish sliding back into a stream, he was suddenly all power and grace. The clumsiness that enabled outfielders to throw him out so easily was gone. His feet churned up a white foam and his small, neat head cut the water like that of a seal.

On this particular day, this Friday, last day of the week, he had hurried at his doglike ramble all the way

Buddy

from school, hoping to get in some swimming practice before the pool filled with yelling kids. He changed to trunks, pinned his locker key to his towel, and stepped through the door to the pool. In one hand he carried the guard's keys on a stick. The water lay smooth, heavy, and green, like a pan of Jell-O. Not a ripple marred the surface. The pool steamed out a strong chlorine smell, the Health Department having recently insisted on adding enough chemical to peel the hide off a small child. The goggles Buddy wore to protect his eyes from the chlorine hung around his neck.

A tribe of roaches double-timed along the baseboards as they saw him coming. Otherwise, no members were using the pool. There were so many cockroaches at the Boys Club that they had honorary membership, and stood in line at the snack bar like anyone else. Disappointed that the pool was completely empty—for the rule was *Never Swim Alone*—Buddy tossed his towel and keys on the guard's chair and padded to the door of the game room.

He stuck his head inside. Two boys were playing pingpong while a third boy watched. This boy wore a loose sweatshirt with the sleeves cut off, and OSBC stenciled on the back. He wore a small black hat with the brim notched into a sawtooth pattern and buttons pinned all over it.

Little Pie

"Hey, Little Pie!" Buddy called. "Howsabout coming in here a minute? I want to rack up a few laps."

"*Simón*," said Little Pie, in Spanish, meaning, *Sure*. His full name was Johnny Pastelito, but Pastelito meant "Little Pie," so that was what they called him. With his glossy brown eyes and almost girlish good looks, he had the sweet face of a young saint. You could picture him in a field with birds landing all over him. But the four blue dots tattooed on his hand told that he had swung with a fighting gang called The Choppers. He had been clean ever since moving to Dogtown, however, and he was one of Buddy's good friends.

Buddy balanced on the edge of the pool, curving his toes on the lip, until he heard Little Pie enter, whistling. As he pulled his goggles up and rolled his shoulders to shake out the muscles, he began to get that good feeling of something fine about to happen. If you kept yourself low in the water, Mr. Hannibal said, your body weighed only five pounds. Think of that! Five pounds.

Buddy took a breath and dived, hard, low, and flat. "*Go, man!*" he heard Little Pie yell. And when he rolled his head for his first breath, he heard him shout, "Five yards' lead and gaining, *amigo!* Go!"

Buddy grinned. Crazy kid always had to be yelling. The funny thing was, Buddy could actually swim faster with Pastelito rooting that way. Reaching the deep end of the pool, he rolled his face up again, his mouth taking the elongated shape of a gasp of air. He started back fast, everything just right, everything smooth.

. . . And that was when this bad thing happened. This accident so bad that, forever after, Boys Club members called the day it happened on, Bad Friday. . . .

The fact was, it had been nip and tuck over closing the Oak Street Boys Club for years. Mr. Hannibal, the director, had struggled and schemed to keep it open. There were problems with the Health people, the Fire people, and the Safety people. The building had been condemned over and over, but Mr. Hannibal had always managed somehow to get a rematch with the rats and roaches and the secret killer called Fire.

The Boys Club and its grounds occupied nearly an entire square block in a very old neighborhood known as Dogtown. Dogtown was too hilly for factories or housing projects, too old for anything but small and usually very poor homes. Because of the hills that ringed it, it was more or less hidden from the rest of the great city of which it was part. But at night the sky above it glowed with the city's lights, as with the glare of an open-hearth furnace, and factory fumes were always in the air.

Over the hills of Dogtown, just the color and shape of potatoes, crawled narrow streets. Down in the flats were schools and small shopping areas, as well as decrepit churches and a couple of dusty parks. Across the north end of the area, curving like a concrete roller coaster, ran a freeway. Motorists on it could gaze down on the tiny houses and wonder what was in them.

What was in them were kids.

Half of the kids—boys—spent their free time at the Boys Club. The other kids, girls, hung around the Girls Club, where they planned dances and things to get the boys over from the Boys Club.

From the freeway, high above, the Boys Club resembled a sturdy red T of tile roofs. The buildings formed a lumpy pile of mission arches and brown stucco walls, set among ratty palm trees. The playground had seen such long, hard use that it looked skinned, like a child's knee after a spill. A motorist up there might catch a frozen instant of action as a big Negro boy got some wood on a pitched ball to sail it *up, up, up!* until the fascinated driver could almost reach out and grab it.

On the club's roof he might see Mr. Hannibal, with some of the boys to help him, replacing cracked tiles. Or there might be a Health Department team in heavy clothing setting poisoned bait in a palm tree for the savage gray rats that nested in the sawtoothed fronds.

The Oak Street wildlife—mostly rats, roaches, and mice—gave the director many headaches. The Health people claimed roaches had been invented there; that an insect known as the Oak Street Beetle absolutely could not be poisoned or gassed. Roaches of this family ate the film in the photo class lab and gnawed the green fuzz off the pool tables.

As for the rats, they were so fierce that they were said to have hijacked garbage trucks and left the crews bound and gagged. Once a crowd of young male rats, according to a frightened night watchman, had stormed through the gym wearing green berets.

Mr. Hannibal had his troubles with the Fire Department, too.

"Paint that old firetrap red and put a fuse in the roof," said the fire marshal, "and I'd arrest you on the spot for illegal possession of fireworks." But he let the place stay open on a strictly week-to-week basis.

The truth was that no one really wanted to shut down the Boys Club. For if the building were demolished, everyone knew that another dangerous animal would crawl from the ruins to roam the streets in noisy hordes. Animals of this variety would eat anything, fight anything, try anything. They had a fierce craving for greasy food, soft drinks, excitement, and games. When bored, the older animals would even trifle with girls.

They were called Boys, and Mr. Hannibal beat the Health people down many a time by saying:

"There'll be more deviltry going on here than you ever heard of before, if you close me up. What's a boy going to do when there's nothing *to* do?"

Then came Bad Friday. What happened to Buddy Williams that day really tore it. Even Mr. Hannibal could not argue that one down. . . .

2
The Thing in the Pool

Buddy was feeling great as he neared the first turn. He heard Little Pie shriek, "Now your fas' turn, man!"

You idiot, Pastelito—you really are an idiot! Buddy thought, grinning to himself as he curled his body through the turn and shoved off again. The goggles gave him the keen vision of a fish. Handfuls of shining air pearls spilled from his fingers as he stroked along. In the concrete floor of the pool, he saw a new crack. And a lost key. A couple of drowned roaches were being teased by suction toward a slotted drain.

"Leadin' the whole pack, man!" Little Pie shouted at the next turn.

Buddy flashed above a bobby pin. Girls got to swim on Thursday nights—a screaming madhouse. His sister, Angie, wouldn't go in deeper than her knees for fear she would get her hair wet and Buddy's friend, Rich Smith, would see her looking just terrible.

Fourth lap. Buddy noticed something like a gray towel stuffed into an overflow drain on his right. Who was being so smart, stuffing things in drains? Or—or *was* it a towel? For now it seemed to be swimming toward him!

He felt a great pulse of fear. The gray thing had a long

sharp nose, small black eyes, and little swimming feet. With horror, he knew what it was. He lifted his head and gave a shriek of terror.

"*Rat!*" he yelled.

He saw Little Pie stare, then start searching for a weapon. Then he ran to the game room. The rat was still coming. Only a few yards away, now. As Buddy tried to backpedal, it swam closer, its small sharp teeth clashing. Suddenly Buddy ducked and swam to the bottom of the pool. But the water was only five feet deep, and out of the corner of his eye he saw the rat swimming right after him. He tried to yell, and lost all his air in a single drowned squawk. Frog-style, he swam toward the far side of the pool. He got a hand on the gutter and started crawling out.

The rat snapped at his foot—actually grazed it with its teeth. Buddy screamed and smashed his fist down on the animal's back. With a twist of its body, it clamped its jaws on his forearm. Buddy went cold with pain and fear. When he raised his arm, the big gray rat clung to it. Dizzy and weak, he began hammering at it.

Then he heard feet slapping along the side of the pool. Little Pie and Rich Smith raced up, shouting. Rich held a pool cue; Little Pie brandished a bronze trophy snatched from the cabinet in the game room.

Thunk!

Someone hammered the rat on the head. Dazed, it fell to the cement floor. Buddy crawled away, trailing blood as bright and red as paint. As he crawled, moaning, he heard the boys smashing the rat to death. Other boys came running in. Then there was the voice of Mr. Hannibal, authoritative as a pistol shot:

"Here, now! What's going on?"

"A rat—a lousy rat!" someone yelled. "It bit Buddy."

Mr. Hannibal took charge.

"Danny," he told one boy, "get the first-aid kit. Pato, call Dr. Otis, and Animal Regulations. Both numbers are on the Emergency card on my desk. Then call the police. Little Pie, stand here at the door and don't let anyone in."

Bad Friday.

Buddy shivered on the edge of the pool, watching his blood flow down the gutter while Mr. Hannibal bound a towel tightly about his arm. He heard a big boy named Cool mutter:

Cool

"Wonder if it was rabid, huh? Man, I guess ol' Buddy kinda had it, huh?"

"No, stupid," Rich snapped. "He'd have to have the shots, is all."

Cool, who could always see the funny side of things, laughed softly. He was bigger and older than most of the boys, a sharp dresser with dark glasses and dimples. He was always popping the iron pills they gave him at the plasma center. Cool sold a pint of his blood now and then for gasoline money for his old Buick.

"What I hear," he said, "dying's almost easier than having the shots. They sticks a long needle in your belly—"

"You can knock that off," Mr. Hannibal rapped. "Get me a couple more towels, Cool. Clean ones. Hurry up."

"Yes, sir," said Cool. "Clean ones."

Cool strode smartly toward the locker room, swinging a fish knife on a long chain.

Even with a guard on the door, boys seemed to come in through the cracks in the walls. Buddy heard a boy mutter:

"Too bad he messed with that rat, huh? The Health people just bound to close us up now, huh?" Buddy did not know who said it, and just then he did not really care.

3
Average Male Cat

Dogtown was a lumpy checkerboard of small homes, blocks of overcrowded flats, and alleys that even scavenging rats entered only in pairs. Patches of decrepit shacks blemished the hillsides. Some of these shacks, nailed together from flattened tin cans, planks, and old billboards, looked so flimsy that, if one fell, the whole row might topple. This end of Dogtown made Buddy think of pictures of Hong Kong in his geography book. People carried water from gasoline stations in buckets and burned kerosene lamps for light.

The Williams family lived in a small, neat home at the foot of one of these clustered hills. Sometimes Buddy felt a long way from the troubles up above, or in the sad and ramshackle tenements west of Ajax Street. Both his parents worked and brought in good money. Yet he remembered a time when his father had been out of work, and the unemployment insurance ran out and they lived for a time in a dirty, rat-infested old building. In Dogtown, no one took good fortune for granted.

Buddy's home fronted a street lined with old camphor and pepper trees. The hill fell so steeply that the garage stood on the street with the house perched above it. Buddy's father had built a rail around the flat roof of the garage so that it could be used as a porch. There was a lawn swing, some wicker furniture, a ping-pong table, and a picnic table where on warm evenings the family could look down, as they ate, on the action of the quiet avenue and squirming Ajax Street, Dogtown's main business street, a few blocks beyond. When one of Angie's boy friends called, she could see him coming and rush inside to touch up her hair and then drift out to say, "Oh, hello, Bobby. When did you get here?"

Tonight the air was warm, with dark coming and a mist of city fumes biting at the streetlights. Buddy noticed that everyone who passed glanced up at the house. He saw a Mexican lady cross herself.

Has Buddy Williams got rabies? they were all wondering.

Rabies! It had always had a rather pretty sound, like "babies." Now it was a dark thing hidden beneath a bandage.

His mother's friends had begun calling as soon as she got home from work at the service center. She had sounded calm and unworried.

"Oh, no, there won't be anything like that," she would say. "No stitches, even. Yes, he's feeling just fine. Thank you for calling, May."

But when she took her place beside Buddy, he could feel her radiating worry. She forced a smile and said, "It doesn't hurt much, does it, dear?"

"No, no," Buddy said seriously. "Feels just fine. I'll prob'ly pick a fight with a rat every week or so."

His sister, Angie, smiled sympathetically. Angie was

sixteen and planned to be a nurse. Buddy guessed she must be practicing on him, because she was trying to be very cool and professional.

"What did Dr. Otis do for you?" she asked.

"Cleaned the cut. Gave me a balloon and a sucker."

"No, really," Angie said, shaking her head. "I'm interested."

"So you're interested," Buddy said. "I'm not."

Ralphie, Buddy's twelve-year-old brother, stared fixedly at the bandage on Buddy's arm. "What's rabies, Mother?" he asked.

"Never mind," Mrs. Williams said. "Ready for dessert?"

"Buddy, what's rabies?' asked Ralphie.

"Something rats have and I don't need," Buddy said.

Ralphie turned to his sister, beginning to pucker up. "Angie, what's—"

Angie interrupted quickly. "Oh, look! The string beans on your plate make a 4. See?"

Ralphie nodded absently, his mind on rabies. He had a special sense for trouble, like radar. "Can you eat rabies?" he muttered.

Angie and their mother got busy trying to get him off rabies. Once Ralphie got on something, he might ride it for days. He had been on Christmas songs and records for years—as long as Buddy could remember. For though he looked like any other boy of twelve, he attended a special class called Point Two, for children who were—well—very slow.

No one seemed quite sure what was wrong with

Ralphie. It was something about a birth injury, Mrs. Williams said, and nothing but love could help. Yet he had a memory that would not quit, and if he had met you when he was two, he would call you by your name ten years later and ask how your brother Sam was—if you had a brother Sam, that is.

Memory! He remembered names so well that when Mr. Hannibal had a special mailing to get out, he would sit Ralphie down with a couple of hundred envelopes and Ralphie would address them without once looking at the mailing list.

How did he do it? Ralphie-magic, Mrs. Williams said. In a special way, the family was very proud of him.

Someone was kicking along through the dead leaves on the walk. "That's Rich Smith!" said Ralphie. "He's

Rich

coming to see me." He bounced up and down on the picnic bench.

Angie jumped up. "Oh, darn! Why doesn't he ever call ahead?" she said.

"He's coming to see Buddy, not you," her mother told her.

The door closed behind Angie just as Rich came trotting up the narrow steps between the garage and the cement wall of the garage next door. He came onto the porch, a lithe, good-looking boy. He muttered hellos and sat down, looking embarrassed. He wanted to know what the doctor had said, Buddy realized, but he was afraid to ask. For all he knew, they might be getting ready for a funeral.

"You're just in time for dessert, Rich," Mrs. Williams said.

Ralphie patted Rich's arm as he sat down beside him. "Hi, Rich! What's rabies?" he asked.

Rich rubbed his forehead and glanced around the table. A little balloon of irritation burst in Buddy's head.

"Judas Priest!" he said. "Give him his records or something, Mom!"

"Rich wants to hear *Rudolph*," said Ralphie, beaming at Rich.

Mrs. Williams took Ralphie into the house.

"What about the, uh, rat?" Rich asked coolly.

"They couldn't save him," said Buddy.

"No, I mean—"

"I know what you mean. They're going to make some

A colorful concept book with die-cut board pages. Ages 2-6, $2.50.

G. LEARNING COLORS WITH STRAWBERRY SHORTCAKE

In an irresistible small format with board pages... toddlers can count on it for fun! Ages 2-6, $2.50.

H. STRAWBERRY SHORTCAKE'S 1-2-3

Classic children's poems in a book that really rocks back and forth! Ages 2-4, $2.95.

I. STRAWBERRY SHORTCAKE'S SUNNY DAY POEMS

© 1982 Random House, Inc.

Bunch of Grapes Bookstore

Main Street
Vineyard Haven, Mass. 02568

Please send the books whose letters are circled below in the quantities specified under each letter:

A	B	C	D	E	F	G	H	I

Name

Address

City   State   Zip

Printed in USA 1/82

☐ Charge   ☐ Check or M. O. enclosed

Please add any applicable sales tax.

Books to Sweeten Every Kid's Day From Strawberry Shortcake and Her Friends

A charmingly illustrated storybook for ages 4-8. $5.95.

A. THE ADVENTURES OF STRAWBERRY SHORTCAKE AND HER FRIENDS

Playtime fun with easy-to-assemble punch-out books! Ages 5-8, $3.95 each, paper.

B. STRAWBERRY SHORTCAKE'S PLAYHOUSE

C. STRAWBERRY SHORTCAKE'S TOY BOOK

Creative coloring and activity books for hours of entertainment! Ages 4-8, paper.

D. STRAWBERRY SHORTCAKE'S MAKE-AND-DO BOOK $2.95.

E. STRAWBERRY SHORTCAKE'S STORYBOOK TO COLOR $1.95.

Enticing smells in a book to scratch and sniff! Ages 2-6.

F. THE SWEET SMELL OF STRAWBERRYLAND $3.95.

tests. The doctor said he didn't think it was rabid, but if it was—"

The music of *Rudolph, the Red-nosed Reindeer* floated from the house.

"Mr. Hannibal got some plinking guns," Rich said. "Cool and Soc Chavez and the night watchman are going to be on duty all night hunting rats."

"What's a plinking gun?"

"Little twenty-two-caliber pistol." Rich cocked and fired his right thumb.

"Little Pie ought to be good at that," Buddy said. "That was a plinking gang he ran with over in Bandini Courts. Couple of his friends plinked themselves into reform school."

Rich put his elbows on the table and squinted at the distant traffic along Ajax Street. Then he sat back and solemnly crossed his arms. Something was bothering him, Buddy saw.

"What's the score?" he asked.

"Well, nothing. Only, after you left I was trying to tell the guys how you got bit. And I guess I'm not sure."

Buddy was puzzled. "You were there, weren't you?"

"Yeah, but when I got there, you were already crawling around with the rat hanging from your arm. —It came out of a drain, huh?"

"That's right," Buddy said. Then, flatly, "What's happening, man?"

Rich passed his hand over his hair. "Some of the guys were saying—you know—'Buddy messed with it; he should've known better. Now they'll close the club because of him.' "

Buddy sat up. "Who said that? Who said I messed with it?"

"Little Pie. I mean that's what I heard. Some of the guys *said* he said it. I don't know. I heard them talking. *They* said that *he* said you were teasing it with that stick you carry the guard keys on. And it ran up the stick and bit you."

Buddy scowled. "Why, the lying—! If that's a friend, I don't need an enemy. His hands better be as fast as his mouth when I see him. —So if the club gets closed, *I* get blamed, huh?"

Rich shrugged. "That's just what I heard, Buddy. Don't blame me."

The screen door squeaked, and Mrs. Williams and Ralphie came out carrying plates. Angie followed with a pie and a serving knife. For a moment Buddy hardly recognized his sister. She had pulled on one of the wigs she had earned the money for by baby-sitting, changed her lipstick, and put on a different blouse. With the part of his mind that was not hot with anger, he thought, *She must be gone on this dude.*

"Oh, hi, Rich!" Angie said softly. "When did you get here?"

"Oh, man!" Buddy muttered.

"Started moving this way when I heard the refrigerator open," Rich said.

Angie laughed and gave him a special smile that made Buddy wince in embarrassment.

"You want to hear a good joke?" Buddy said. "Little Pie's telling it that I teased that rat and made it bite me."

Mrs. Williams laughed. "How silly!" She passed Rich some pie, then frowned. "You *didn't* tease it, did you?"

"Oh, sure! I've got all these fingers, see, and a guy doesn't need more than a couple on each hand." Glumly he shook his head. "It just goes to show you. You can't trust a bean."

His mother looked up. "That's enough 'bean' talk. We say Mexicans, not 'beans.' Besides, I don't really believe Little Pie would say it. You don't have a better friend than Johnny Pastelito."

Buddy knew it was true. They could spend hours together and never get on each other's nerves. Most of the time they spent laughing, just because they felt so good. Yet if Little Pie were spreading a story like that, he'd have to believe he had never really known him at all. He felt tricked and disappointed. In a way, he wished Rich had not told him. Bad news about friends would always keep.

Rich spoke suddenly to Ralphie. "Hey, Ralphie! There's going to be a membership meeting tomorrow. Mr. Hannibal wants you to address envelopes while we hold the meeting. Okay?"

Ralphie twisted on the bench in excitement and began reciting:

"*List A! Contributing Members; Alcorn, Howard, 432 Alpine Street. Andrews, Clayton—*"

Rich grinned. Over Ralphie's voice, muttering List A

members, he said that a meeting was being held in the morning to discuss the whole mess. The club would have a better chance of *staying* open, Mr. Hannibal thought, than of getting opened again once it was closed.

"—*Atkins, Harriett, Estate of, 110 Hilltop Road*—"

In his brother's mind, Buddy knew, the whole glorious day to come was unrolling—a full day of addressing envelopes. Anything Ralphie could do well he would cheerfully do forever. And in that spectacular, mixed-up brain of his there was stored, on some kind of tape, every name of any importance whatever to the Oak Street B.C.

"Estate of Harriett Atkins," said Buddy's mother suddenly. "Has anyone checked on Buzzer Atkins lately?"

Buddy and Rich looked at each other. Sparks of excitement crackled in Buddy's head as he thought, for the first time in months, of the rich old tomcat sitting on more money than most people in this world would ever get near.

An old lady named Harriett Atkins had left her cat, Buzzer, a half-million dollars when she died years ago. On Buzzer's death, the money was to go to the Boys Club. But the cat, attended by a high-priced vet and a full-time caretaker, showed signs of living forever. In the lobby of the club hung a dusty chart made up years before:

LIFE SPAN OF AVERAGE MALE CAT

A black cutout on a graph showed Average Male Cat climbing the trellis of the years, like a tomcat stalking a bird, to fail suddenly, with one forepaw on 13 and the other on 14, where Death, in the form of an automobile, a dog, or a seizure, struck him down.

AGE OF BUZZER ATKINS

was the heading of a similar graph. It showed Buzzer at Age 28, and, so far as anyone knew, still in the very prime of his life.

"Mr. Hannibal keeps track of him," Buddy said glumly. "That old cat will outlive all of us."

"But if he ever does die," said Rich, "who's going to tell us? Old What's-His-Name, the caretaker, keeps him locked up out of sight."

"Buzzer lives up there," Ralphie said, pointing toward the highest hill in Dogtown.

Everyone glanced up at the line of hills that fenced Dogtown in on the east, behind the Williams house. Though it was nearly dark, Buddy could make out the bony ridge of the hills, broken by power poles, a reservoir, and a cluster of trees where Buzzer's mistress had lived and where now Joel Shriker, who had been her chauffeur, lived with the cat.

Once he had gone up there with some other kids. They had not been able to see much because of an iron fence that surrounded the place. It was not just any fence, but the kind with spear points from which you could imagine yourself hanging by your intestines if you tried to climb over. All they could see was that the big house was boarded up and that someone was living in the guest house. Sometimes they would see the caretaker driving through Dogtown in an ancient, glittering Hudson.

"If I were Mr. Hannibal," said Buddy's mother, "I would certainly check on that cat. It's a crime that an old tomcat should live like a king, while boys that should have a new club are being bitten by rats."

"Well, one thing's sure," Angie said brightly. "If the club *does* get closed, you boys can always come to the Girls Club for dances and parties. In fact, Gail and I were talking last night about having a couple of dances a week this summer—"

"You going to have boxing and swimming too?" Rich asked.

"No," and Angie laughed, "but maybe there'd be room for a few boys in our knitting class. And there'll be a hair-styling class this summer."

Rich got up. "Thanks, I'll probably keep styling mine with clippers. Thanks, Mrs. Williams. 'Night, Angie. Meeting's at nine thirty, Buddy. Don't forget to bring Ralphie."

"*List D!* Ralphie shouted as Rich swung down the steps to the street. "*Active Members . . .*"

4
Is Buzzer Atkins Dead?

Two hundred of the club's thousand-plus members packed the game room the next morning. Most of the younger boys were out playing somewhere or still were at home. At one end of the room was a little platform. Shelves of musty books, the club's library, lined the wall behind a long Masonite table where Mr. Hannibal sat with Buddy, the secretary; Rich, the Boy-of-the-Month; Robert Hankins—known as Cool—sergeant at arms; and two other older boys.

Buddy had a dark feeling as he sniffed the homey odors of mothballs and insecticide, plus a whiff of chlorine from the swimming pool. He had grown up here, as most of the old-timers had. The club was where you were when you were not somewhere else. And where else was there to be?

But it was all over with the Oak Street B.C. now. If he had been a dog, he would have pushed his nose at the ceiling, and howled.

In the audience, Little Pie caught his eye and winked. Surprised, Buddy winked back, then remembered he might have to cream him for spreading that story. But, on the other hand, hitting anybody, member or not, got a boy suspended. Life was complicated.

Mr. Hannibal rose and tapped a pencil on the desk. "All right, boys, let's get started."

A rubbery wave of movement swept the folding chairs, some of which folded at every meeting. The boys raised anxious faces to the director. They came from homes where pure Spanish was spoken; where Negro parents had once followed the crops; from white homes where skin was no problem unless folks got democratic and lay too long in the sun trying to turn brown. Some of the kids, Buddy knew, had police records; just as many were on the Honor Roll.

In the Boys Club, it made no difference what a boy had been. Only what he was now, or was trying to be.

Solemnly, Mr. Hannibal gazed out over these boys he loved, who loved him; and Buddy had the feeling he was having trouble getting started. Mr. Hannibal looked tall and distinguished, with his crisp little gray-black beard cut square at the corners. He wore a blue blazer jacket and gray slacks. Sometimes he made Buddy think of an African delegate to the UN. Tapping a pencil was all he needed to control a whole roomful of boys, though Buddy had seen teachers yell themselves hoarse and get nowhere.

"I'm glad to report," Mr. Hannibal said into the quiet, "that hunting season opened last night. Robert Hankins bagged three buck rats."

At the table, Cool shook his clenched hands above his head. He crunched on an iron pill.

"Did you tease 'em first, Cool?" a boy called.

Buddy's head snapped up. Boys were grinning in a

ripple area around Socrates Chavez. Soc played dumb, but Mr. Hannibal said sharply:

"Step out in the aisle, Soc. Get going on fifty push-ups."

Soc grinned, ducked his head, and lay down in the aisle. He made thirty-two pushups before he expired, groaning.

"You can work out the rest later," said Mr. Hannibal. "If I hear any more talk about Buddy teasing that rat, fifty pushups won't even touch what's going to happen."

Little Pie glanced at Buddy, then gripped his knees and shook his head. Buddy could not decide whether he looked guilty or not.

Now the room was quiet. Buddy had the feeling that Mr. Hannibal did not know how to express what he had to say. A cold feeling iced up his insides as he watched the director's fingertips pressing the tabletop.

Mr. Hannibal cleared his throat. "Most of us," he said, "have known this old club for a long, long time—"

There it was.

It was all over with the Oak Street B.C. In silence and in sorrow, the boys listened as he explained. A sadness like mustard gas rolled over the stricken crowd.

The club, he said, would be padlocked this afternoon.

"However," he added, "I'm trying to make arrangements to use a playground only a mile or so from here for games. And the public plunge will be open next week, after school is out. And there's the Southwest YMCA, of course—"

Open to boys of all races, Buddy reflected—providing

you had twenty dollars in your jeans. If there were five kids in your family, then your folks had to get up a hundred bucks.

The Boys Club was a dollar a year. If you didn't have it, you could work it out. All over the hall, boys were groaning.

". . . As a stopgap," added Mr. Hannibal, ruffling his little beard with his knuckles, "I'm trying to raise money to have the place fumigated again. Ralph Williams is addressing envelopes to sponsors right now. Hear him?"

The growing mutter of unhappy members hushed. *Clickety-click-click, click, click.* They heard him.

"Let's have a hand for Ralphie, how about it?"

The boys cheered and clapped, then were quiet. Buddy was pleased. Of course, what Mr. Hannibal had been after was quiet and good feeling. Ralphie was an afterthought. Raising both arms, Mr. Hannibal said heartily:

"I count on you fellows to live up to the Boys Club code till we're back in business. You're all my boys, and that makes you brothers, doesn't it? And if I hear about any of you brothers throwing with each other, or anybody else, I'll ask for your membership cards. Now let's do the code: 'I believe in God and the right to worship according to my own faith and religion. I believe—' "

A few of the folding chairs folded as the audience stood. Yet there was no laughter or horseplay. In four sentences, the code built a fence a kid could not crawl under or over. It hemmed him in with such good intentions and good feelings that he was proud to be trapped there. *Whoever wrote it,* Buddy thought, *knew boys— that any kid would much rather be good than bad.*

Afterward, Mr. Hannibal asked the officers of the Keystone Club, the older boys' special group, to stay for an emergency meeting. Buddy stayed, along with Rich, Little Pie, and Cool.

Mr. Hannibal closed the doors of the big game room. Through the office door, Buddy heard the typewriter clacking. Ralphie was now reciting the code as he typed.

Poor Ralphie. *Going to kill him,* he thought, *not getting to help Mr. Hannibal anymore. Poor me and Angie too, stuck with him all summer. We'll all be mental cases by fall.*

Mr. Hannibal hung his coat on the back of his chair and sat down. By this gesture he told them it was something pretty special, something just among them.

Buddy opened the notebook in which he kept the minutes of the Keystone Club meetings, but Mr. Hannibal shook his head. "No, this is a secret meeting. No minutes."

Their glances ran around the circle. Well, well! Secret meeting! The low feeling in Buddy began to rise.

"All right," the director said. "You four are the Buzzer Atkins Committee—my Keystone Cops. You're going to find out whether that old tomcat is still alive."

Cool grinned. With his big black sunglasses he looked like a blind man without a tin cup.

"Loan me that plinking gun again," he said, "and I guar'ntee you he won't be alive tomorrow."

"And I guarantee *you*," retorted the director, "that we'd never see that money. We'd have a lawsuit that would go on forever. Besides, I don't regard cat killing as a proper activity for Boys Clubbers, do you? You're going to be detectives, not hired assassins."

Cool said he was just kidding, and turned on a humble expression. He popped another red iron pill.

Mr. Hannibal patted the tabletop with his palms as though it were the back of a pet. "Guess," he said, "how much money is in the Estate of Harriett Atkins now?"

"Fifty grand!" Rich blurted.

"Guess again."

"Hundred grand!" Cool yelled. The others scowlingly shushed him, as though by such foolish talk he might put a hex on the whole thing.

"According to the last annual report of the Trustee," said Mr. Hannibal, glancing at a paper, "there was $639,843.96."

Buddy's head swam. Little Pie whispered something in Spanish. Cool put his hands on top of his head.

"Man, you could build *ten* Boys Clubs for that kind of bread!"

"No—just one. But we'd have a real club. And by George, if that Buzzer cat is really dead, and we're being cheated out of the money, it's got to be the crime of the century."

"Why don't you call the police?" Buddy said. "Then

you could all just drive up there where he lives, and eye-ball things."

"Because Joel Shriker won't let me in. He's the care-taker, you know. I called a few months back and asked leave to examine Buzzer. Nothing doing, Shriker said. Visitors excite the cat, he claimed. Bad for an old cat's heart."

"Man, that dude is full of it!" snorted Rich. "He's living the life of Riley up there. You seen those powder-blue uniforms he wears? They must cost two hundred dollars—of our money."

"Shriker gets a good home, all expenses paid, and a fat salary. Plus, we're losing at least $500 a year to the vet, and a nice chunk of cash to Mrs. Podesta, the lady lawyer that's the Trustee. She runs the show, you see. She says what he can spend and what he can't spend, and just between us I think he's kicking back about half his salary to her. But the day Buzzer dies, they're all plumb out of work."

Cool pushed his glasses up to the top of his head. "We got to go to court, then," he said. "If the judge says they've got to show us the cat, that's it. —Ain't it?" he added.

Mr. Hannibal shook his head.

"Going to court costs money. Mrs. Podesta and Shriker would fight us. Might be two years before we got inside, and by that time I'd be long gone from here. I've got a job offered me in Cleveland that I'm going to have to take if we don't open this can of peas real fast.

Whereas if we can prove on our own that the cat's dead, we might be able to close Shriker out overnight."

"That old woman musta been crazy," Rich said. "Leave all that loot to a cat."

"Maybe. She had *four* cats when she died. Buzzer's the only one left. I remember meeting her once. . . ."

Mr. Hannibal crossed his arms and looked at the ceiling. They waited.

"She came down from her hilltop in that big old Hudson. It was new then, same car Shriker drives to this day. And the neighborhood was newer too, not so rundown as it is now. Miss Atkins looked the plant over and went away. I never saw her again. But when she died, Mrs. Podesta called and said we'd been named in the will and she was the Trustee."

"Mrs. Podesta is a white woman, huh?" Cool said.

"Yes. But Shriker's a Negro, so it leaves us up a tree for which race to blame. You talk about weirdos! That Mrs. Podesta is a card-carrying nut. She's hung up worse on dogs than Miss Atkins was on cats. I've called on her, and I take a vow she had two hounds in her office and a whole station wagon full in the parking lot! She showed me an album full of dog pictures and played me a tape of them barking, for background music! That's the solid truth. By the time I left, I'd forgot what I went there for. Didn't know B from Bull's Foot. But I did get the message that if I came messing around, she'd invoke a clause in the will that says if anybody contests it, he doesn't get *anything*."

Gloomily, he glanced at a paper. "I get these annual reports on the Estate, as an interested party," he said. "Look at this: *'False tooth for Buzzer:* $350.00!' I can't afford that kind of dentistry myself, boys. I called Mrs. Podesta about that one. She said he's called Buzzer because he bit an electric cord when he was young and the spark killed the nerve of a tooth. Miss Atkins got him a false tooth, and it fell out a while back and he had to have a new one."

Gloom settled over the table like dust. All that money going down the drain.

How come he called the meeting? Buddy wondered. *How can we find out if that cat's alive, if he can't?*

Mr. Hannibal fingered his little frosty-black beard.

"Boys, I want you to get me a picture of that cat," he stated. "Then find an old newspaper picture of Buzzer when Miss Atkins died. And then we'll know."

Buddy laid his arm across Rich's shoulder.

"That's you he's talking about, brother," he said, smiling. "Winner of the Best Picture contest."

Rich shivered. "Not me! That little trophy I won isn't getting me over any iron fences."

. . . One Saturday during the contest, Rich had followed a man down Ajax Street, secretly snapping pictures as he stole things from unlocked cars. A newspaper had printed the pictures, and the contest committee gave him the prize for the best picture of the year.

"Who's talking about climbing fences?" asked Mr. Hannibal. "I'll borrow a telephoto lens for you. All you'll have to do is lie in the weeds outside the fence and wait for Shriker to bring the cat out for exercise."

Nothing to it, Buddy thought. *For somebody else.* But it was spooky up there—the big house shuttered since the old woman's death. The shrubbery was dusty and overgrown. Nothing had been kept up but the little guest house where the cat and the caretaker lived.

"Well, what do you say?"

Rich shrugged. "Okay." Cool removed his heavy sunglasses, squinted at them, put them on again, and said, "Hey day! Okay." "*Simón,*" said Little Pie cheerfully.

Buddy sat there digging a thumbnail into the eraser of his pencil. "Well, Buddy?" said Mr. Hannibal.

"I was just thinking. . . . If we're going into combat together, I ought to know my friends from my enemies." He gazed into Little Pie's saintlike features.

Little Pie stared back. He knew what Buddy meant. He said flatly: "I didn't start that talk, Buddy. Maybe Soc—"

But Mr. Hannibal cut in. "I don't think any one boy started it, Buddy. The fact is, when something bad happens, people have to find someone to blame—just anybody."

"Ain't that the truth!" murmured Cool.

"You know that's so, Buddy," Little Pie said.

Rich nodded. "That's a fact, isn't it? I never thought of that."

At last Buddy grinned. "I'm glad you guys are taking it so well. I'll be big about it too. Let's have a skull session at my place tonight, and we'll get moving. When can you get that lens for Rich, Mr. Hannibal?"

"I'll call Charlie Motley, at the *Times*, about it today, and ask him to bring it to your place first time he gets the chance."

5
"Shotgun Traps Set!"

Along Ajax Street, the lights of Saturday night burned in the city mist. Buddy gazed out over them from the garage-top porch where the family had just finished dinner. Neon signs and taillights stained the mist like his blood in the swimming-pool gutter after the rat fight. There would be hooting and hollering in the bars tonight. Cars would get smashed up, and certain intersections would be sprinkled with broken glass as naturally as dandruff on a coat collar. No one but the police and the victims would pay much attention.

But in houses like his, things would rock along about the same as ever. For example, his father, a parole officer for the Adult Authority, was home early and they were all discussing the sad state of the Boys Club.

"So they really locked the old firetrap up this time," said Mr. Williams.

"For good," Buddy said.

"Maybe Mr. Hannibal can get permission to fumigate it again."

"Maybe. But the pest men said last time that the rats must wear gas masks, 'cause they never saw vermin come back so fast."

"Where's Ralphie?" Angie asked, in sudden concern.

"In the kitchen, probably, looking for something more to eat," said Mrs. Williams. "Relax, baby."

Angie shrugged. She had a special sense where Ralphie was concerned, Buddy had noticed. She acted sometimes as though he were her son instead of her younger brother, and nobody had better say M.R. in her hearing. M.R. meant Mentally Retarded.

Suddenly there was a snuffling sound in the doorway behind them. It was Ralphie. He came and went like smoke—saw all, knew all, though on a slightly different plane from other people. Sometimes, carrying his head slightly to one side, he seemed to peer at the world through a crack in reality, so that he saw things in a way others could not.

Buddy realized that Ralphie was crying.

"Buddy's going to die!" Ralphie sniffled.

Buddy felt a cold draft. His brother had something like the gift of prophecy: he would just as soon be left out of his guesses.

"Heavens!" Mrs. Williams laughed, opening the screen door. "He must have heard me talking to the doctor."

Ralphie came out and sat down, his face torn with grief. He looked at Buddy mournfully.

"Is somebody trying to tell me something?" Buddy asked, suddenly uneasy.

"The doctor said it's *all right*. The rat didn't have rabies."

"Why don't you let me in on these things?"

"I was saving it for after dinner." Mrs. Williams kissed Buddy, then put her arms around Ralphie. "He said the rat was in perfect health. It had lived like a king over there and even got regular exercise. It was in beautiful condition, except for having been beaten to death."

A horn honked. Buddy took a handful of cookies and headed out.

"Where are you going?" Angie asked.

"Cruising."

Before he and the boys had broken up today, they decided to start their investigation of the Buzzer Atkins mystery right on his doorstep. They were going up tonight to look things over.

In the car were the three other members of the committee. Cool turned the car up a steep street into Dogtown Heights.

The hillside below the old Atkins estate was an avalanche of castor bean plants, pepper trees, palms, and magnolias pouring down the slopes. A little pot was grown here and there too, behind rank hedges and broken fences. Out-of-plumb shacks stood on tiny lots. Buddy caught the tang of supper fires as they drove along a winding lane called Lopez Street. Broken glass sparkled in the headlights.

"Slow down," Rich told Cool. "That's Sultana Street coming up."

"Better park near the corner," Buddy said. "It's only a block up the hill."

Cool stopped under a shaggy old pepper tree. As he killed the engine, the noises of Dogtown's Saturday night rose from the little valley of lights below them. Horns honked; a few dogs barked; somewhere a siren was screaming like a frightened woman.

"Lookee!" Cool said. From under the seat he pulled a strange contraption: a length of brass pipe, a cap-gun trigger, and a curl of spring with a rivet in it to act as a gun hammer.

"Put it away!" Little Pie said. "Man, you're out of your head to pack that around."

Cool pursed his lips and juggled the zip gun on his palm. "One shot from this cannon, and that old cat—"

"One shot and the *club's* dead too," Buddy retorted. "You heard Mr. Hannibal."

Cool sighed and stowed the gun out of sight.

They all gazed up the steep dirt road. Just where it joined Hilltop Drive, at the top of the ridge, stood a dark grove of trees. Somewhere among them a light shone through tangled branches.

They climbed, two boys on either side of the road. As they reached the top, an engine whined behind them, tires scrambling for traction in the gravel.

"Car coming!" Rich barked.

Buddy flopped behind a bush that smelled like the black flea soap used on pets. He could hear small stones being flung back by spinning tires. Was it Shriker coming in the big old Hudson? He trembled with mortal fear of the man. Though he had scarcely talked to him, he had seen him on Ajax Street for years, getting a shine or going into a bar, a solid, thick-necked man in a pale-blue uniform and a black chauffeur's cap.

Shadows reeled and ran as the automobile's headlights broke through the brush. Choked by the pounding of his heart, Buddy clutched the ground. He squeezed his eyes shut. *If I can't see him, maybe he can't see me.* Then he opened them, disgusted at his fear. A white station wagon as long as a hearse was passing. Dogs were barking in it. He heard a woman cry, "Boys—behave!" But she was talking to the dogs.

She drove on, swung left down the narrow paved road at the top, then into a long driveway. *Mrs. Podesta, I'll bet!* he thought. *The lawyer woman with all the dogs.*

One by one the boys stood up. Suddenly Little Pie gripped Buddy's arm.

"Meet you up there! He's going to open that gate for her. Works by electricity. I'll see if I can—"

Can what? He was gone, running like an antelope. What a character! Buddy stepped into the road and started after him at a jog. The others followed.

They stole up a graveled drive through the dark trees. Yard lights flooded a sweep of yellow lawn behind an iron fence. At the rear of the lawn, on the left, stood a large old house with the doors and windows boarded up. Near it, scarred like an old fighter, stood a twisted oak tree. To the right of the main house sat the caretaker's cottage, trim, newly-painted, with lights burning behind the windows.

Suddenly there was a most awful uproar of barking dogs. Buddy started in surprise, then moved closer to the fence to see better. The fence was a wicked-looking barrier of spears set upright in iron joists. The gate moved on a little rail, so that it could be opened and closed electrically from the house. Near the gate, he saw Little Pie lying in the shadows.

There seemed to be dogs everywhere, large floppy-eared hounds the color of mice, prancing and racing. *Thank the Lord for that fence*! he thought. Shriker stood with his hands on his hips, watching the dogs frolic, a big panther-like man with dark-oak-colored skin. He wore a black T-shirt and blue uniform pants, and looked like some sort of special cop. A woman all in black stood near him, contentedly swinging a little chrome leash. She wore black glasses, black slacks, and a black sweatshirt with a hood thrown back. Even black gloves!

Mr. Hannibal was right. She was straight from Weirdsville. A huge dog leaped on her, and she would have fallen, but for Shriker's steadying her.

"Oh, you lovely boy!" she cried to the dog. "Aren't you the lovely boy? Joel, isn't Rex a lovely boy?"

"I reckon," Shriker said, in a deep voice.

Suddenly, out of the corner of his eye, he saw one of the hounds digging in the earth under a window. He swept up a small stone with a swift movement and hurled it. The dog yelped and took off.

Mrs. Podesta cried angrily, "Joel! Now, see here—!"

"I'm sorry," said the caretaker. "But did you see what he was doing?"

"Yes, but . . . Oh, I see," Mrs. Podesta said.

Some sort of message seemed to pass between them.

"Maybe we better kind of herd them up," said Shriker. "I don't want Buzzer getting all upset."

"Of course not. I have some new pictures of Lady Grace to show you, too," Mrs. Podesta said. "Here, boy—"

Buddy signaled to Rich and Cool. This was the time to move in close, while the caretaker chased the dogs, penning them one by one in the wagon. The boys crawled up and lay near Little Pie.

"I got the gate jammed with a stick!" Little Pie whispered. "The stick kept it from closing. If he turns out the lights, we can ease it open and crawl through."

"With all them hounds?" Cool whispered.

"They'll be in the car. Can't smell anything but each other."

"Seen the cat yet?" Buddy panted.

Little Pie pointed through the grillwork of spears. "Look in that window and tell me if that's not a cat laying there—"

Buddy stared. It was! He was positive. A neat cat shape lay on a windowsill in a room at the right end of the guest house. Silently it seemed to watch the action, not letting on that it was there.

"If he don't ever let him out," Rich muttered, "I can't get a picture even with a telephoto lens. Not even in daylight."

"How come?"

"Not enough light in there."

"How about a—what-you-call-it—flashgun?" asked Cool.

"Flashgun big enough to light the house from here would burn it down," said Rich.

Gloom settled like smoke. Rich dug in the earth with a twig, pondering.

"If I had a real long extension cord—"

"Yeah?" Buddy urged.

"—And one of you guys Injun'd up near the house with the flashgun— I don't know, though," Rich said. "I'd have to run a cord from the gun to the camera, and there'd be lots of resistance in a wire that long. Might have to use open flash. Have to ask Mr. Motley—"

Without warning, the floodlights died.

A screen door banged. Buddy saw two forms cross a window. The cat shape on the back window rose, stretched, and jumped down.

"Let's go!" Little Pie whispered.

They rose silently and drifted up to the gate. Buddy tested it. It slid back on its oiled track. But as he held it open, Rich whispered:

"Wait a minute! What's that sign say?"

A little board was wired to the gate. Cool pushed his face close to it and spelled out:

" 'Shotgun—Traps—Set!' Holy cow!" he gasped.

6

The Caretaker's Cat

"It's only just to scare people," Buddy said. "And anyway she just drove through, didn't she?"

"Yeah, okay. But I'd feel better if—" Cool slapped his neck as though a mosquito had bitten him.

With a gesture of disdain, Little Pie jeered:

"That's an old gag. Like putting a note on your beer when you go to the john: 'Don't drink this, 'cause I spit in it!' "

And he walked in through the gate.

Buddy caught his breath; but nothing happened. It was just a gag. *This little guy's got class*, he thought. *He's not afraid of anything. Glad he's on my team.*

He saw Cool pop a couple of those Midnight Mission pills in his mouth for courage and walk through the gate. Buddy and Rich collided in the opening, neither wanting to be last—nor to be left alone in the dark.

Silently they moved toward the cottage. The dead lawn felt like sponge underfoot. In the night there was a choky smell of dry grass, a lemony fragrance of eucalyptus trees. Buddy shivered with excitement. A voice cried as they neared the little house:

". . . But what trouble could anyone make for you,

Joel? You have every right. Is that, or is that not, Buzzer Atkins on your lap?"

Buddy sagged. *There's your answer, Boys Clubbers!* he thought mournfully.

Buzzer lives.

But for some reason the caretaker did not at once reply. "Well, uh, uh—well, yes," he said. "That's true. Isn't it?"

He did not sound very sure of it.

"So how could they make trouble?" asked Mrs. Podesta.

In the car, there was a snapping and snarling of ill-tempered hounds. Buddy slid close to a window and looked into the cottage.

Mrs. Podesta sat in a chair with a cup of coffee steaming on an end table beside her. She had removed her sunglasses. She had fair, shiny skin with eyes pushed back into her skull like pale-blue marbles in dough. Her hair was pulled up into a knot, and quite a bit of it straggled loosely. On her lap lay a photograph album.

"I mustn't stay," she said, "but I wanted to set your mind at ease. The fact that the Boys Club has been closed *in no way* affects your position here. You see that, don't you?"

Shriker, big as a tree, looked odd petting that little old cat. His huge hand half covered Buzzer; though, for a cat, he was big too. He was a mostly-black cat, with one white ear, one black. His coat gleamed like varnish. He probably ate better than ninety percent of the kids in

Dogtown, Buddy reckoned. Though the tomcat's eyes were closed, his head was raised alertly as Shriker stroked him. If you knew cats, you knew that in a split second he could be ten feet away, spitting and clawing.

He ought to look good, thought Buddy. *That there is a half-million-dollars' worth of tomcat.*

"I was thinking," Shriker said, "that we might let *some* of the money go to the kids. You know—enough to get 'em started—build 'em a pool or something— kinda stall off bad feelin's—"

Mrs. Podesta, her faded blue eyes glittering, shook her head. "Oh, I couldn't permit it. It would be *very* bad legally. It would seem to say that you felt guilty about something. You don't, do you?"

"No. Why should I?" Shriker grinned, and shook his head. In the lamplight his face was the color of an old pigskin billfold. Big and lean, he made Buddy think of a panther. *Don't want to tangle with that dude, ever,* he thought.

All at once Shriker's eyes raised to the window. He seemed to look right at Buddy. A sort of instant Ice Age froze him. His blood chilled. But of course it was dark here and he could not really—

Shriker's face distorted. He set the cat on the floor and leaped up.

"Kids!" he roared. "Kids peeking in!"

They turned to run.

"Let the dogs out!" Shriker was bawling. "Let 'em tear them kids a little. Teach 'em—"

"No!" cried Mrs. Podesta's voice. "They might have a gun—hurt my lovely boys—"

The voices faded. Everything faded but fear, and the *thunk-thunk-thunk* of pounding feet; then sliding the gate open and racing down the driveway. Skidding into Hilltop Drive and down Sultana Street. Somebody falling. "Owww!" Buddy helped him up—Cool.

They reached the old Buick and scrambled into it. Cool stamped on the starter button. W*ow-wow-wow*— the starter went slowly; then slower and slower. Everyone sat forward, praying, one or two who had not prayed in years.

. . . W*ooow-Wooooooow*—

"Been having some trouble—weak battery—"

A car slid into the rutted dirt of Sultana Street and raced down the hill.

"Get out and push! Get her started downhill."

It was no use. They had just got the car turned downhill when the white station wagon braked beside them. The dogs were going crazy. Buddy piled into the car, the others behind him. Swinging into the Buick's path, the lawyer-woman forced Cool to stop. Shriker jumped out and came around to the driver's side. His hard, tan face shone with sweat.

"Young sirs!" he said sternly. "Something you wanted?"

A good man in a tight, Cool steadied down.

"You could give us a push, mister," he said.

"I could give you all a smack in the mouth, too," said Shriker. "What were you doing on my property?"

"Don't even know you, mister," Cool said. "You live up here, huh?"

"I'm Joel Shriker. The man that you were just peeking into his house."

"No, *sir*," stated Cool. "We just parked here to look at the lights."

Shriker turned and gazed down at the lights of Dogtown. Turning back, he thumped his fist against the door of the car. "Ain't they pretty?" he said. "But, I'm telling you, kids, you'll see lights that'll fade those a mile if you ever come back. Because I'll mash you every way there is. I've got two big fists, and—"

"No, Joel!" cried the woman gaily. "They're sorry—don't threaten them. Aren't you sorry, boys?"

All the time, the dogs were shrieking and roaring.

"Sorry about what, lady?" Cool called.

"Oh, come on, Joel," Mrs. Podesta snapped. "Don't lower yourself to their level by bickering. You'll just have to reset those shotgun traps, I suppose—"

Shriker straightened, pulled his mouth down, and glared at them. "—Every way there is," he repeated. He walked away.

7
The Great Duck Robbery

Buddy's father was eating a late dinner on the porch when the boys came trooping up the steps from the garage. Though it was Saturday, he sometimes had to make a call on his own time to be sure that one of his old boys, as he called them, was not getting into a mess. Though some of his boys were fifty and sixty years old, he had a fatherly feeling toward them quite different from a policeman's toward a parolee.

"You can't help feeling sorry for these old recidivists," he said once.

"What's a recidivist?" Buddy asked.

"A loser," said Mr. Williams. "Just a loser."

As they passed him, Cool had his hands clenched so that his skinned palms would not show. He had said there was no medicine at home. His mother was working nights now, and his father hadn't been around lately. With all that dirt ground into the flesh, Buddy had insisted on his coming home to have the cuts cleaned.

Mr. Williams glanced up over his glasses, a gray-haired man given to wearing bow ties. He looked more like a professor than like a parole officer. His glance flicked over them, and he said, "Hello, boys. What happened?"

"Nothing, Mr. Williams," Cool said, grinning and bobbing his head.

Buddy sighed. Since his father *expected* people to lie to him, you really hadn't a chance. So he told most of the story, while the boys sat down at the picnic table and Mr. Williams continued eating.

"Lois," Mr. Williams said finally, "have we got some peroxide? Robert has some cuts here that ought to be cleaned out."

Mrs. Williams took Cool inside the house. Ralphie sat by his father. When had he come out? Buddy wondered. The mystery boy. He came and went like a ghost.

"Of course you know you were trespassing," Mr. Williams said.

" 'Shotgun Traps Set,' " Ralphie said softly.

Mr. Williams dropped his fork. "What?" he asked.

Ralphie repeated it, while Buddy rolled his eyes up. He had forgotten. Ralphie had gone up there with them one time. Buddy had not even realized his brother had read the sign.

" 'Shotgun Traps Set,' Rich," Ralphie said happily.

"Uh-huh," Rich muttered.

"I gather," Mr. Williams said, "that you entered in defiance of a sign that warned you to stay out, and threatened your lives? Is that it?"

"Well, it didn't really say 'Keep Out.' Just that about traps."

"And you took that to be a sort of invitation?"

"No, but—"

"I understand why you've got to move quickly on this, boys. But getting your heads shot off wouldn't be quickly. Do you plan to go back?"

Buddy glanced at Little Pie, who took off his sawtooth hat, rotated it ninety degrees, and set it down again. "Got to, Mr. Williams," said the Mexican boy. "Got to get a picture of that cat."

"Well, you saw it, didn't you? Can't you sketch him from memory? Then compare it with the newspaper photo at the library?"

Rich pulled bits of rubber off his tennis shoes. "He had a black right ear, and a white left one. And—"

"Black *left* ear, you mean!" Little Pie said.

Buddy closed his eyes and tried to see the cat. *Black left . . . Black right . . .* He was sure it was a black left. But he was not positive, if that made sense.

They were all waiting for him. "*Seems* like it was a black left ear," he said, "but, man, when Shriker let out that yell, I forgot everything!"

"So you're back where you started," said his father. "The gun-traps sign is an old dodge, and it's illegal. But if there *is* a gun trained on that gate, 'twon't matter whether the law was on your side or not when it goes off."

Rich stripped some more rubber from his shoes. "I got a telephoto lens coming up," he said. "If I can figure a way to get some light on the window, I'll have it made."

"I'd suggest lying low for a while. Whatever you do, don't go back into Shriker's yard. Tomorrow you might go to the downtown library and see what you can find in the old newspaper files."

"Tomorrow's Sunday," Buddy said.

" 'Shotgun Traps Set,' Little Pie," Ralphie said, picking at the sleeve of Little Pie's T-shirt.

"Uh-huh," Little Pie said. Suddenly he stood up. "*Ahí te huacho*," he said. It meant, *See you around*, Buddy knew. Then he was gone.

"What got into him?" Cool asked, walking from the house with gauze on his hands.

"Don't know," Buddy said. "Little Pie burns with a short fuse."

What had got into him, he knew, was that Ralphie made him nervous.

From the distance came a *skeeeee-wham*! of automobiles colliding. Hardly anyone looked around. Saturday night in Dogtown.

"That miserable Grover Street underpass," said Mr. Williams. "I'll have to write the City another letter requesting a signal."

"Want to gimme a push?" Cool asked the boys.

They went down to the street and pushed him until the engine fired. In this end of the city, they called that a Dogtown Starter.

Sunday morning.

Buddy had never cared much for Sundays. You ate too much and there was nothing to do. Between meals you drank Cokes and ate fried stuff from plastic bags, and belched. Cells went dead in your brain until it ran down like Cool's battery.

By 3:00 P.M. of this day, he was bored; sick of Ralphie's prattle, too. Ralphie played *Rudolph the Red-Nosed Reindeer* and *Christmas Chopsticks* for a solid hour, and when Buddy yelled at him he went to his room and cried quietly in the closet. Mrs. Williams told Buddy he knew better, and Angie said he should be ashamed.

A *whole summer of Sundays*! Buddy thought dismally.

The phone rang for him.

"You want to go over to Eastlake Park?" Cool asked. "I got a charge on my battery this morning. Pastelito and Rich are going."

Buddy's mother said it was okay if he took Ralphie.

"He'll be fine," she assured him. "He's just bored. Take some dry Jell-O along in case he gets restless. —I'll give you some money for rides."

Twenty minutes on the freeway plucked them out of Dogtown to an area on the opposite side of the city's clanging heart. Tall apartment houses lined a wide boulevard. There was an S-turn where a boulevard snaked through a small park. On a little lake, electric-powered motorboats cruised gutlessly, being passed even by showoff ducks. Among the big old trees were a few rides, tame ones like the dodge'em cars; nothing that made you wish you'd let your lunch settle before blast-off.

They wandered the shore of the lake. Ducks waddled ahead of them, and they threw popcorn to the birds.

"Wonder if these ducks migrate," Buddy said. "Seems like they're always here."

"What's 'migrate'?"

"Fly south."

"If I was a duck," Cool said, "I'd migrate to Mexico. Have me an auto-body shop. My uncle was in T-town—that's on the border—for a while. He says those beans are good mechanics, and they only get a dollar a day."

Buddy saw Little Pie's back straighten. Cool was unaware that he had said anything wrong. A Mexican, Little Pie was technically a bean.

"I got a dollar," Buddy said hastily. "Let's rent a boat for a half hour."

But the boat man wanted a ten-dollar deposit, so they went over to the dodg'ems. Everyone got in a car. Ralphie and Buddy teamed up. There was some bad feeling—just a little cloud in a blue sky—when Little Pie kept slamming into the back of Cool's car. He nearly tore his head off, once. He was sticking it into him for saying "beans," Buddy knew.

This will be the longest summer in history! he thought. *And it hasn't even started.*

They climbed a smooth-barked tree until a policeman chased them down. Ralphie was beginning to pester for something to eat, so Buddy gave him a box of Jell-O. One of his hang-ups, Ralphie ate it dry; but the doctor said it was probably good for him. He would eat only green Jell-O, and that made his mouth green, and embarrassed Buddy when people stared at him.

They sat on a little footbridge high above the water while Ralphie ate. A fleet of ducks paddled by under them.

" 'Four ducks on a pond,' " Ralphie said to himself. " 'A grass bank beyond.' "

"When's the plunge open?" Rich asked.

"Week from tomorrow. Now that the club's closed it'll be a madhouse. Need a shoehorn to get in the water."

It was quiet except for Ralphie licking waxed paper, and a little boat humming beneath the bridge.

"This ain't none of my idea of fun," said Cool gloomily.

"What's your idea of fun?" Little Pie challenged.

"A club."

"It's closed, stupid."

"Our own club, I mean. We had a club when I lived in Bunker Heights. We called it the Jokers."

"A gang, you mean."

"No, not a fighting gang. We did things like, uh, like set flares in the road. Then we'd watch cars try to figure out whether they could go by. And turn on fireplugs. And shoot out streetlights."

"Big times," said Little Pie scornfully. "Gang I was in, in Bandini Courts, the Choppers, was a fighting gang. We'd throw with some gang every couple of weeks."

"What kind of gangs—grammar school kids?" Cool sneered. His neck must still be sore from the dodg'em, Buddy knew. And now he realized something was up.

"Gangs of spades," said Little Pie. "Like you."

Cool started to get up. Little Pie was already up. Buddy gripped Cool's shoulder and pushed Little Pie away.

"All right, cool it!" he said. "You said 'bean,' Cool. I know you didn't know it, but you bad-mouthed him just the same. Now he's bad-mouthed you—us too, but forget it. I've got a better idea than a club. An idea that'll get us in the paper!"

Cool and Little Pie were still squared off to each other.

Rich asked, "Yeah? What's that?"

"It will be dark in an hour or so," Buddy said. "We're going to take one of those sacks out of a trash barrel. Then we're going to migrate some ducks."

A grin broke the line of Little Pie's mouth. "How we going to catch 'em?"

"Wait'll it's dark. I'll show you."

8

Saint Buddy, the Martyr

Teamwork was what greased it. Buddy was the underwater demolition man, Rich and Cool the sack men, Little Pie the stakeout man to watch for park patrolmen. Even Ralphie had a job: he was camouflage, and he stayed with Little Pie. Obviously, the Mexican boy was taking care of a retarded child for someone, so he could be up to no mischief. Oh, obviously.

The trash sacks were emptied just before dark, so there was no disposal problem when the boys collected sacks. Inside each hinge-topped barrel was a canvas bag, so that the whole barrel did not have to be lifted when it was emptied. The men just lifted out the sack.

Beneath a bridge, Buddy stripped to his underwear. He swam along a rushy bank, only his head above the water. Ahead of him, now, he saw a little huddle of mallards near a bank. They had their heads tucked under their wings. His sack men trailed him along the bank, far enough away not to disturb the ducks. Buddy glided up to one of the ducks, scarcely breathing. Then he reached forward, found its feet, and pulled the bird under the water.

The other ducks swam off. He got nipped by the

duck's bill as he clamped his hand over it. Then the fight was over, with hardly a murmur of noise. He stood up on the oozy bottom and carried the duck to the bank. Cool, going on pure inspiration, slipped a rubber band from his wrist over the duck's bill. The sack men stuffed the duck in the trash bag as Buddy went after another.

Within an hour, the boys had two sacks of ducks—eleven mallards, only eleven over the legal limit.

Cool moved his car around to the side of the park and they stowed the sacks in the trunk. Stifling their laughter, swatting their thighs, they headed off.

"Where we going to migrate them to?" Cool asked.

Buddy sniffed the odor of moss rising from his body. It had not been as much fun being a UDT man as being a sack man, but he had prevented a fight.

"Patton Park!" said Rich.

"Where's that?"

"Bandini Courts," Little Pie said. "My old neighborhood. Listen, I don't know about Patton—"

"It's perfect!" said Cool. "A little bitty lake and no ducks on it."

He swung the wheel and headed southwest.

A gap-toothed line of small factories blocked the park on the north. Buddy remembered Patton Park as a very poor one. With the lights out except along a few paths, it looked uninviting. The lake was a mere pond. Yellow trash barrels were the prettiest thing about Patton Park. The drinking fountains stood in murky puddles; there was some climbing equipment of blackening pipe frames; chicken-wire frames protected some small trees the park department was trying to keep alive. With a city haze drifting over it, Patton Park resembled a battlefield more than a park, and the bronze general standing near the street with a sixgun in each hand and a World War II helmet cocked to one side seemed to be defending it against all comers.

They sneaked the sacks through the shrubbery to the edge of the lake. Ralphie, refusing to stay in the car, kept muttering, " 'Four ducks on a pond,' " until Buddy snapped at him. Then he whimpered. It was getting late for him, and Buddy wished they were home. He did not like the shadows and the strangeness. It was gang country, too, and they should have listened to Little Pie.

But they giggled as they released the indignant ducks. Then they drowned the sacks with a rock in each so that no one would link them up with the Great Duck Migration. They made so much noise that when they turned to leave and suddenly saw the group of boys on the path watching them, Rich uttered a yelp of surprise.

"*Pinacates!*" a boy said in Spanish.

"*Tintos,*" said another.

Buddy tingled. Catching his fear, Ralphie began to cry. The boys were small, but their voices were deep. In Spanish, they made remarks that finally brought a response from Little Pie.

"*Te doy safos,*" he said. Once he had explained that phrase to Buddy. *Try and stop me,* it meant. Then he said some other things and started walking toward them. The boys backed like a pack of little wolves. Just as wary as wolves, and just as dangerous.

"Stay with me," Little Pie muttered to the others. "These guys are rough. They're the Cobras—"

They stuck close. Buddy peered into the faces of the boys on his side of the path. They appeared to be sixteen or seventeen years old. One of them wore a little high-crowned hat with no brim. All wore tight black pants and T-shirts. He saw no weapons yet. The boys stopped backing, and blocked the path.

"*Oye, Chacón*," Little Pie said. "How you doin', huh?"

"Hey, that's Pastelito!" one of the Cobras said. "You running with bloods, now, huh?"

"These are my friends from Dogtown," Little Pie said.

"Chihuahua!" One of the gang kids laughed. "You really hard up for friends, man."

"We got to be going," Little Pie said. "Say hello to the mob, huh?"

Buddy's nerves twanged like guitar strings. They started walking toward the gang boys. To his surprise, they parted to let them pass. Ralphie was crying.

"Muvver! I want Muvver!" he sobbed.

"Hey, look, a dum-dum!" said the boy with the brimless hat. "Hey, Dum-Dum, what's your name?"

"Leave him alone, Chacón," Little Pie said. "Come on—"

Chacón grabbed Ralphie by the shoulders and wrenched him around to the streetlight. "*Mire!* His mouth is green! You live on grass, man?" he asked Ralphie. "You smoke your pot green?"

"Let him go!" Buddy snapped. A fierce anger rose in him. But he knew that if he started anything, there would be a big fight that they would probably lose.

Ralphie still held a half-eaten packet of Jell-O. Chacón tore it from his hand and shook it over Ralphie's head. "Now you look sharp, Dum-Dum, now you—"

Whap!

Chacón reeled back and fell onto a bench. Buddy felt a sharp pain from the punch he had thrown. He had hit Chacón so hard in the mouth that he thought for a moment he had broken his wrist. In the streetlight, blood made a clown's mouth of Chacón's lips. Dazed, he looked up at Buddy. Another boy jumped on Buddy from behind, slashing at his face with a beer-can opener. Little Pie yelled a Spanish curse at the boy and seized him by the wrist. The can opener jabbed Buddy's cheekbone. Buddy swung his left fist around low and sank it into the boy's belly. The boy started making sounds as though he were going to throw up.

A man shouted. A spotlight tore through the shrubbery from a cruising automobile that had stopped with a squeal of tires. Then a red gumball machine atop a police car began to revolve, and a policeman leaped out and came charging up with a nightstick in his hands.

The Cobras scattered like quail, even the hurt ones.

The dazed Dogtown boys stood there. The truth was that they were willing to be arrested just to get out of this end of town. Bandini Courts made Dogtown look like a summer camp.

When the police headed them toward the car, Buddy saw that Little Pie had vanished also.

9
Bug Crew

"Any you kids got priors?" asked the sergeant.

It was four o'clock Monday afternoon. Last night they had been released to their parents, except Cool, whose parents could not be found. He had been released to Buddy's parents. Juvenile Division was upstairs in a very old police station with pipes and wires like vines on the walls, and the same old pale-green paint every police station in the world seemed to have. At least according to Cool, who had seen the inside of a few.

The boys shook their heads. No prior offenses.

Downstairs, their parents waited with Mr. Hannibal. The police wanted to question the boys without parental interference, first, Captain Provo said. Mr. Hannibal said it was illegal, but they were doing it anyway. The captain was sitting by listening, while Sergeant Sanchez, a juvenile officer, and a very stout officer named Sergeant Swann conducted the questioning.

"No motor vehicle violations?" asked Sergeant Swann. He was eating a snack at his desk, a very wet French dip sandwich in a paper basket. He never looked up as he questioned.

No, sir. No MVD's either, the boys said.

"What were you doing in that part of town?

There was grease on the sergeant's chin. It bothered Buddy, who could not keep his eyes off it, waiting for it to form a drip.

"Just looking for something to do," they said.

"Something like a gang fight?"

"No, sir. Just—just anything."

"No priors, eh?" Sergeant Swann glanced up keenly.

"No, sir!"

"Not me, Sergeant."

"Me neither."

The sergeant dropped his sandwich in the basket. His face reddened as he roared:

"What about gang fighting, Hankins? What about truancy? What about malicious mischief?"

Robert Hankins—Cool—took a step backward, startled.

"I been—I been—I been clean since I come to Dog-town, Sergeant! And those old raps—I didn't think— see, I did my—"

"Yeah, we know you did, Hankins, or you'd be on your way to forestry camp right now with a shovel in your hands. When I ask you something, I want the truth. Is that clear?"

A telephone rang. "Get that," Captain Provo said, looking up from some papers he had been reading. "It looks like counsel and release, Sanchez," he said to the other juvenile officer.

"I think so."

"Send the parents up."

"That other guy too? Boys Club man?"

Captain Provo shrugged.

Sergeant Swann took another bite of sandwich as he listened, then talked in a garbled fashion:

"She's trying to *poison* you, Mrs. Walters? Oh, that's too bad. Your sister-in-law should know there's a law against poisoning. But she keeps right on putting electricity in your soup, eh? I'll tell you what: we'll send a man over after a while, and you can explain it all to him."

The parents came in. Buddy was humiliated for his father—a parole officer who could not keep his own boy in line. But they had told the truth. The only thing they had not told was what they were doing in Patton Park. Mr. Hannibal wore a coat of shame with a clear stripe of anger across it. *He'll really give it to us later*, Buddy thought.

Ralphie, slicked up and wearing a bow tie like his Dad's, looked excitedly at all the desks, radios, and telephones. Probably, Buddy figured, he thought it was Santa Claus's headquarters.

Fanning himself with a Wanted notice, the captain told Buddy's and Rich's parents how things stood.

"Maybe it was self-defense, as the boys say. I think these are pretty good kids. That's why I'm releasing them with only a warning. But I do wish they'd stop lying about what they were doing there."

"Thank you, Captain," said Mr. Williams. "Thank you very much, sir."

" 'Four ducks on a pond,' " Ralphie said, hurrying up

to look into the division commander's face. " 'A grass bank beyond! The blue sky of spring,' Captain—"

" 'White clouds on the wing,' " said the captain, to Buddy's astonishment. "That's a nice song, son. My mother used to sing it."

"Isn't that nice?" said Mrs. Williams, tears of relief standing in her eyes. She didn't want her boy to have a rap sheet. As much as anything in life, Negro mothers in Dogtown prayed that their boys might grow up without a bad sheet of charges to keep them from ever getting a good job.

"That old song," said Captain Provo, "reminds me of a story I read in the newspaper this morning. It seems that some of the ducks in East Lake Park migrated to Patton Park last night. Isn't that amazing?"

"We did it; we did it!" Ralphie chortled.

Everyone slumped and looked at his feet.

"What else did you do, son?" asked Sergeant Swann sharply, rising like a bulldog. Ralphie looked at him, and whimpered. The division commander swiveled in his chair and stared at the detective.

"Will you for— Why don't you just finish your lunch, Swanny?" he asked. He shook his head. Then, to Ralphie: "You all had a good time, eh? Did you bore holes in a boat, too, maybe?"

"No. Just ate stuff. 'What a wee little thing,' Captain—" Ralphie said, and waited with a big smile.

The captain closed his eyes and recited slowly: " 'To

remember for years. To remember with tears. To remember for years . . .' "

Buddy had not breathed since Ralphie's confession. How many years would he have to remember—with tears—those ducks? Mr. Hannibal chuckled.

"Everyone's reciting so nicely," he said, "that I'd like to ask these boys to recite the Boys Club pledge. I just wonder if they can fit duck-napping into it somewhere. All right, Captain?"

The captain waved his hand.

The boys recited the code right up to, " '. . . I believe in fair play, honesty and sportsmanship.' " As much as any of the *I believes*, that one nailed them up like thieves. Buddy had hit somebody first, too, and that was worth a suspension any day of the week. Would Mr. Hannibal get it out of him?

Mr. Hannibal, looking more than ever like a United Nations delegate, said:

"I'd like to keep these boys believing in such American ideals, Captain. But it's going to be hard with the club closed. Impossible, perhaps. That's what prompted this shameful little episode, at least to some degree. The knowledge that their summer had to be crossed like a desert."

"I heard about your trouble, Hannibal. It's tough, I agree. It may be tough for us, too. But—"

"I've applied to the national organization for help, and I'm sure I'll get some. How much, I don't know. I'm contacting all our sponsors, too. At any rate, if we could only stay open through the summer on some temporary basis—"

"Fumigation again?" asked Sergeant Sanchez. "That old shanty's been fumigated so many times it smells like a bug bomb now."

"I know, but it's the only way to keep operating. And by September, maybe we'll have our finances in hand."

"What do you want me to do?" asked the captain. "Try to square things with the Health Department?"

"Would you?"

"I'll call them today. But they don't regard me as any more of an expert than they do you, so I have no idea what they'll do."

"If you would, Captain—!" Mr. Hannibal said fervently.

As they filed out, Buddy heard Sergeant Swann telling Sergeant Sanchez:

"These people all want something for nothing. I never saw anything like it."

"Uh-huh. By the way," Sanchez said, "you owe me sixty-five cents for that sandwich."

10
Fat Cat

On Thursday afternoon Mr. Hannibal called the Williams home. As she always did, Angie took the call. She came back to the porch where the boys were playing poker with matchstick stakes.

"Mr. Hannibal's coming over. He has a camera lens for you, Rich. What are you going to do with it?"

"Take pictures of broads at the beach," Cool said, licking his lips. He drew a deep breath and pushed his chest out.

"You don't have to be crude," said Angie. And Rich shook his head disgustedly.

"This guy's a mental case. Huh!—not a bad idea, though, while I've got the lens. You point out the girls, I take the pictures—fifty cents."

Mr. Hannibal trotted up the steep steps from the street without even breathing hard. He worked out strenuously every day, and the way he felt about smoking was that he'd almost rather a boy smoked pot than cigarettes.

"At least it doesn't crud up your lungs," he claimed. "Only the mind."

He sat at the picnic table and opened a paper tube he carried. Inside was a leather case; within the case was a black metal tube with chrome trim.

Rich handled the telephoto lens with reverence. "I hope this thing's insured," he said. "You could prob'ly buy a car for what this is worth."

"Practically. Mr. Motley says you have to hold the camera absolutely steady. The slightest motion will ruin the picture. You *should* use a tripod, but under the circumstances—"

He frowned. The circumstances, yes . . .

"I hope you fellows know how I feel about asking you to do this. It isn't for me, really. The fact is, I don't really expect to be here next fall anyway."

Buddy was shocked. The way they felt about Mr. Hannibal, the builders had stood him in a field and built the Boys Club around him.

"I've got to get lined up with a job pretty quick. I called Cleveland, Ohio, and there'll be an opening there in August. If things aren't settled here, I'll have to take it."

"Then we've got to move!" Buddy said. "Where's your camera, Rich?"

"Not so fast." Mr. Hannibal smiled. "Give Joel Shriker's nerves a chance to settle. You've got some investigating to do at the public library before you go any further."

Guilty looks flicked from boy to boy. Cool cracked his knuckles like walnuts.

"See, I don't have a card. So I can't go there."

"You don't need a card unless you take a book out," Angie said. "Anyway, Rich has a card. Don't you, Rich?"

"Well, er, see," Rich said. "I don't have bus fare down there, and the little Dogtown branch wouldn't have back copies of newspapers. So—"

Angie laughed. "Cool will take you. What's the *real* reason you don't want to go?"

"I've got a two-dollar overdue fine from last year," Rich confessed.

"And I lost a book a couple of years ago," Cool said. "It was a six-dollar book on sheens. I'm on their Most-Wanted list, I reckon, and I *know* they got this-here 'Bad List,' and they look up your name before they let you out of the building. So I'm *staying* out!"

"I'm clean," Buddy said, "except that Ralphie tore up a picture book once and they probably wouldn't want me messing with their newspapers."

"Oh, well," Angie said, "I'll go with you tonight, if you're all afraid of librarians."

Mrs. Williams called her to help with dinner. Buddy guessed there was no way out of going. Mr. Hannibal was still smiling.

"Those librarians won't give you any trouble. I've known them to have boys shanghaied off the streets just to get them started reading. A dollar a head for captives. You know what they pray every night? 'And, Lord, send a nonreader into the children's room tomorrow so I can hook him on books.' While you're there," he added, "look up 'cats,' in general. How long they live—what their main diseases are—like that."

He got up to leave. Buddy could still see a special cop sliding out of the wings to put the arm on him for being a member of the infamous Williams Family of book destroyers.

"By the way," Mr. Hannibal said, "come around to the club tomorrow—after school. They're going to put the biggest tent in the world over it, and pump it full of gas. Fumigation day! We open again next week."

Cool bounded up and called down the steps after him.

"Then what's all this jazz about pictures and liberries and stuff?"

"When did a fumigation ever last over two months before?" Mr. Hannibal called back.

The downtown library was in a handsome building across the street from the post office. The boys wanted to walk up and down in front of it for a while, and kind of case things; but Angie breezed right in like a taxpayer. The heavy glass doors opened ahead of her, as though they had seen her coming. The boys hurried after, not wanting to go in alone. The fact was that there *was* a Bad List, and marshals had even come to the homes of kids who lost too many books. Buddy wasn't sure whether they came for the kids or the books.

There was scarcely a sound in the place. The ceiling was high, and underfoot was a floor of polished cork tiles. On the left, people were checking out books; to the right they were returning them. A great deal of money seemed to be changing hands.

"Where do we go?" Rich said out of the corner of his mouth.

Buddy was aware of a uniformed guard watching

them near the door. Cool pointed him out with a nod, then said hastily:

"I forgot to put anything in the parking meter. Meet you at the car."

Angie caught his hand. "You don't have to—it's after six."

She walked up to a man behind a desk with a sign on it. *Information,* it said.

"We want to see some old newspapers," she said politely.

"Papers? How far back?"

"Nineteen-fifty," Angie said.

"Go upstairs to the second floor, then left to the end of the hall. Tell the lady at the desk what you want."

On the way to the stairs, they came across an elevator. They all piled in. As soon as the doors closed, Rich began arguing heatedly.

"You know what's going to happen, don't you? They're going to want to see all our cards!"

Angie smiled and touched her hair. She seemed to enjoy being five-feet-three and in command of three large boys. "Don't worry," she said. "I'll take the blame. I'm clean."

"Clean! You're crazy!" Cool muttered. He juggled his long fish knife nervously. "Listen, here, though. Long as we're inside, we ought to look up a book on poisons. More'n one way to research a cat."

"You walk up holding that knife and ask for a book on poisons," Buddy said, "and bells are going to start ringing all over the place."

The elevator stopped; the door slid back. The boys backed farther inside, but Angie walked out with her head high, and they followed. Down the hall was a room with a sign over the door:

Periodicals.

They entered. It was a large room with many reading tables occupied by old men who looked like immigrants. Many wore beards. The papers hung in racks, and you could carry a paper to a table and read. Along one wall were four big machines resembling photographic enlargers. They had pale-green glass screens in the front just like television sets. An old man with a beard and a skullcap was reading a paper that, by some magic, was cast upon the screen. He would turn a little crank and the page would change.

"May I help you?"

A librarian was standing at their elbows. She was young, had blond hair done in a roll, and was smiling. Buddy tensed. The smilers were the worst kind. They feinted you out of position. Then, *Bang!*

Angie explained what they wanted. The woman went behind a counter. She flipped up a card and placed a pencil on it.

"We have all the *Tribunes* back to 1940," she said. "They're on microfilm, and you view them at one of those machines. Do you have some identification?"

"I have a Girls Club card," Angie said.

You idiot! Buddy wanted to blurt. *She means like a driver's license.*

But the woman merely copied Angie's name and her membership number onto the card. "About what year?"

"Nineteen-fifty," Angie said. "We think about April."

Carrying a little roll of film to one of the reading machines, the librarian explained how the thing worked.

"Pull this lever first—it lets you feed in the film. Put the end of the film in the slot, then turn the crank to go forward or back, you see? Use this handle to select the part of the page you want. And if you swing the screen toward you, the page gets larger."

It turned out to be a panic. You cold crank the film slowly and race through *Sports, Society, Classified, News of the World, Comics.* Angie got stalled on *Society.*

"*Look* at those *hemlines!*" she giggled. 'Six inches above their ankles! And their hair—"

They went further.

"Look at that sheen!" Cool exclaimed. " 'Packard Super. Electric clutch.' An' that Roadmaster—looks like it was going to eat motorcycles, all those chrome teeth in front."

The librarian tapped her pencil on the desk, but kept smiling. *That's once,* Buddy thought. *Next time she'll phone the cop downstairs.*

"There he is!"

Angie dropped her hands in her lap. On the green frosted glass was a picture of Shriker with an armful of cats. Below it was a caption:

FATTEST CATS IN TOWN

"Held by Joel Shriker, five pets of late millionairess, Harriett Atkins, grin like proverbial Cheshire cats. They should! They're worth a hundred thousand dollars apiece."

In the center of the army of cats Buddy made out Buzzer. His right ear was black, his left ear white. His nose was white, and the balance of him was hidden by a mess of other cats.

Angie took a pencil from her purse and wrote down the date and the page number. She carried the roll of film back to the desk.

"How can we get a picture from one of the papers on this roll?" she asked.

"You'd have to call the *Tribune*. I don't know how long they keep negatives."

They left.

"Maybe we don't need a picture," Cool said as they reached the street. "We know his right ear's black. All we got to do is get a look at him, and if it ain't the same cat, we blows the whistle on Shriker."

"And they're going to believe us?" Rich said. "Man, you been on stuff? We need *two* pictures—one from the paper, the other of old Buzzer laying in the window. And I'm makin' book we don't get either."

Downstairs, Angie found a book called *Your Cat: How to Care for It*, and checked it out on her card. There was no trouble. Though the library maintained a Bad List, she seemed not to be on it.

11
War on Bugs, Inc.

Little Pie had been scarce lately, but Buddy caught up with him at the lunch stand Monday, where he was swatting bees with his button hat. The bees swarmed around the lunch stand, and if you weren't careful you got beeburgers.

"Where you been?" Buddy asked him. "Haven't seen you since you bugged out at the park that night."

"Been around."

"Not around me. *K.I.?*"

K.I. was a Spanish phrase Little Pie had taught him. It meant, *What's the matter?* Just those two letters: *K.I.*

He guessed they must be spelled some other way.

"I stayed around the house for a couple of days. Those Cobras may be little, but they're meaner than fire ants. Me running with you is the worst thing I could do, way they figure it. I'm glad it's not like that in Dogtown, but there's nothing to keep them from coming over here looking for me."

"I'm sorry we dragged you into it. I figured I'd better try to keep you and Cool busy till you stopped sniping at each other."

"So what's new?" Little Pie said.

"The club's going to be fumigated again Saturday!"

"No kidding!"

"Come around Saturday. They're going to put a big tent over it and gas everything in the joint."

"Maybe I ought to invite the Cobras to the party," Little Pie said. "Lock them in the basement and not tell anybody till it's over. . . . How come a tent? Thought they usually went in with gas masks, like World War I."

"This is a different outfit. Mr. Hannibal got a better price from them. *War on Bugs, Incorporated*, it's called."

The week pulled out like taffy, sagging in the middle. Things were getting ready to happen, but not yet happening.

Ed Motley, the newspaper photographer—he taught the photography class for the club—got a print of that old newspaper picture for them. It looked like the cat they had seen on Shriker's lap, sure enough. But he did not look much younger then. Too bad cats did not get bald, the boys sighed; they'd have Shriker with the goods. But of course the caretaker would have bought Buzzer an expensive hairpiece.

One day Cool saw Shriker carrying a shotgun and a box of shells from a hardware store to his big old Hudson. The committee dropped the idea of crawling across the lawn with a flashgun. For six hundred thousand dollars, maybe he meant business after all: he was going to rig up a trap.

Rich borrowed a bow and some arrows from the club's

archery department and started Secret Experiments. They were so classified that he would not let even the other committee members watch. But it was known that he went to a spot under the freeway, with a bag of flashbulbs, and practiced for hours every afternoon.

Suddenly school was out!

Bad news, thought Buddy. As *bad as it came*.

Any kid who had been through a normal Dogtown summer knew that all but the hardest-core dropouts would be pounding on the schoolhouse doors in August, trying to get back in. Dogtown was not exactly an amusement park. When you had drunk your gallons of charged water and eaten your tons of potato chips, had your boredom-fights, and worn out the sidewalk on a few corners standing around—

Man, you were ready for anything, even school.

And this would be no normal summer, unless the fumigation really took for a change. The Health people would probably assign a man to do nothing but watch the club for rats. And when Rat One showed his nose and whiskers, the place would be locked again—for good.

Saturday morning, everyone in Dogtown who could walk was down at Oak Street to watch the extermination people work. Buddy and some other boys sat on top of Cool's sedan, watching the action.

"Those guys are better than a comedy team," Cool said. "Bet Mr. Hannibal's putting us on. This is really a comedy act."

They laughed as the enormous tentlike tarpaulin rose

halfway up for the second time, hauled by block and tackle, and fell back, trapping two workmen under it. They roared as the canvas lumped and wriggled with the trapped men's efforts to crawl out. There were only half as many workmen as were needed, it seemed to Buddy, but for some reason they managed continually to get in each other's way.

Finally they hoisted the tent over the clubhouse and staked it down all around. Then the workmen all got busy unloading big cylinders of gas from their battered old truck. Each cylinder was rigged up to a tube fixed in the canvas, so that when they were all turned on, the gas would be released inside it.

A little man in white overalls and a turtleneck sweater, who seemed to be in charge (if that were not too strong a term), stepped up beside a cylinder near the sidewalk. He raised both hands for quiet.

"It's a put-on," muttered Cool. "This is too good. Ain't I seen that guy on T.V.?"

"Folks!" shouted the little workman, smacking the cylinder with one hand, "Please give me your attention! Guards will be on duty all night to prevent anyone's accidentally entering the tent. But please spread the word far and wide to *stay away*! In a short time we will fill this tent with gas. Deadly cyanide fumes will destroy all forms of life inside the building. . . ."

"Cyanide!" Little Pie said. "Just like in Death Row. Bet the rats get out an appeal."

"Now, the danger of leakage is slight," continued the foreman. "However, it will take over an hour for the cylinders to empty, and please bear in mind that their contents are under very high pressure." He smacked the cylinder again for emphasis.

Bang!

Sssssssss!

A valve had opened. The man in the white overalls hit the ground and began crawling. A gas like snow burst from a hornlike nozzle. Snowflakes swirled and fell.

"Get away! Get away!" he screamed, waving one hand as he crawled.

Another workman ran to the truck as the crowd broke up with shouts. Then, pulling on a gas mask, he hurried to the cylinder and managed to shut it off. He looked for the foreman, who had reached the flagpole and now clung to it, as though it somehow meant safety or a new record set for flagpole-reaching.

"Gus—" the workman called to him, removing the gas mask. "It's okay. It's just CO_2. That was a fire extinguisher."

As the man in the white overalls sheepishly got up, there was a long silence, then a roar of laughter that must, Buddy thought, have awakened Buzzer Atkins from a sound sleep.

"What do you think?" he asked. "Is it really a comedy team? This is too much."

"Who's hiring comedy teams in Dogtown?" Cool said. "That tent alone would cost a fortune to rent."

"That little guy in the white overalls!" Little Pie gasped. "He's killin' me!"

The little man was hurrying around speaking to each

workman, like a field marshal ready to lead a charge. Each man rushed to a gas cylinder. A few minutes later, on a signal, each gas cylinder was opened. In the hush, a muted hissing was heard, like a den of snakes rattling in the club. The workmen ran around getting in each other's way and opening more cylinders.

Two police cars arrived. Over a bullhorn, an officer ordered everyone to move along, get going, this was not a show.

That was all *they* knew about it!

The crowd drifted off. Television would seem tame tonight.

Very late that night, when only the drunks were still out, banging up their cars and getting arrested, a fireball rose above Dogtown. The unearthly light woke Buddy. He stared out the window. A pear-shaped cloud of violet gas ascended gracefully. Then a soft clap of thunder shook the house. Frightened, he piled out of bed.

There followed a splintering roar. Shreds of flame soared into the sky. For a few instants all of Dogtown stood out, as though in the light of a gigantic flashgun. Then the light faded.

What went on?

Buddy ran to wake his father, but collided with him in the hall. "Dad, Dad! Did you see that?" he gasped.

"It woke me up," said his father. "What was it?"

At that moment the telephone rang, as high and shrill as the screech of a carbon drill. Mr. Williams turned on the light in the kitchen and answered it.

"Oh, hello, Rich," he said. "You can see it? What was it?"

A moment later, taking a deep breath, he nodded.

"Well, that figures. I just can't believe it. But it figures. Thanks for letting us know."

He hung up and looked at Buddy.

"The Boys Club just blew up," he said.

12
Feathers and Flash

Dogtown was sick.

Rat-infested, roach-ridden, it was the victim of a wasting disease known as despair. When the Boys Club blew up, the hopes of a thousand members were shattered with it. You could have shaken this end of the city by the heels, and not a smile would have fallen out.

Nothing to do.

Nowhere to do it.

Let's go over to Bandini Courts and look for Cobras.

Let's shoot out streetlights.

Let's raise some loot busting parking meters.

Let's roll winos.

Nickels-and-dimes stuff, man. Let's steal car radios. Ever sniff glue?

You mean this week?

Before the end of the first week of vacation, nearly all these remedies for boredom had been tried by some bag or other in Dogtown.

Cool was making a long-range, high-performance zip gun to kill cats with. He said he was going to practice on all the stray cats he saw, and when he was ready—

Rich telephoned Buddy in the middle of the second

week. The smoky city dusk was coming down like a fog.

"We'll pick you up in ten minutes," he said.

"What's happening?" Buddy had seen little of Rich lately. He had been practicing with the telephoto lens, he said. Rich hung up. Ten minutes later Cool honked, and Buddy ran down to the street.

The boys were all whispering and beckoning him into the car. Excitement charged the old Buick. In one small area of Dogtown, at least, the sleeping sickness had momentarily passed.

Trailing fumes, clattering like a crippled Sherman tank, the car dragged away. Buddy saw a bow, with the Boys Club insignia on it, and a quiver of arrows on the floor. Rich had a brown paper bag in his lap.

"Where we going?" Buddy asked.

"Bandini Court," Little Pie said. "We're going to shoot Cobras."

"No, come on," Buddy said.

"He ain't telling anybody," Cool said. "We're going over to the freeway and practice archery. Don't ask me how-come, ask him."

At the end of Palm Street—an alley lined with fences of flattened tin cans and scraps of old billboards nailed together—the freeway soared along on thick-ankled concrete legs. A chain link fence with *Keep Out* signs hung on it guarded the State's right-of-way. There was nothing of interest beneath the booming freeway, nothing but tin cans and sun-starved weeds, but because of the fence and the signs, people had gone to great trouble to tunnel from freedom to imprisonment. Once there, they sometimes built little fires, dropped a few pills, drank a little wine, and wrote dirty words on the freeway supports. An old wino was found dead there one time. On a scrap of paper bag he had written his two-word review of the world:

"Everything stinks."

Dusk had thickened almost to darkness as they crawled under the fence. Little Pie read some of the new messages on the concrete.

"How about this one?" he called. " 'Mixed marriages don't work.' Signed, 'Peter, Paul, and Mary.' "

Rich led them to a little hill a hundred feet up the line. It billowed beneath the freeway and sloped into a ridge. A splintered sheet of old plywood had been propped against the steep slope. A rectangle with crossbars had been painted on it in black. It looked like a jailhouse window.

"There's Buzzer's window," Rich said.

"And them holes," Cool said, "are arrow holes. And I thought you guys didn't want to kill him. Somebody's been snowing me."

"Nobody's talking about killing him. See where most of the holes are? *Above* the window. I had to get the range. I've got a sight on this bow just like a rifle, crosshairs and everything."

"So what's the use of a sight, if you're not going to shoot something?" Buddy asked.

Rich led them back to where he had left the bow,

arrows, and paper bag. After stringing the bow, he emptied the bag on the ground. It contained a very small battery about half the size of a boy's little finger, plus some tiny camera flashbulbs like ice cubes. An arrow had been fitted with tin clamps into which he squeezed the battery. Then he taped a flashbulb just ahead of it. Finally, he connected some wire.

"With a big enough bow," he said, "I could take moon shots."

"Yeah, but can you take pictures here?"

"Works every time. When the arrow hits, the battery slides forward and hits this wire. That makes the bulb go off."

He pushed the battery a half-inch. The bulb ignited with a frying sound and a dazzling flash. Rich turned the flash cube to expose another set of terminals. Each cube could be flashed four times.

"Can you hit anything with all that stuff on the arrow?" Cool asked.

"I had to learn how much lift to allow," Rich said. "But watch this."

Planting himself at right angles to the target, he fitted the arrow to the string. With his left hand gripping the bow, he drew the string back. He locked the arrow in position with one knuckle pressed against his jaw, holding the position so long that Buddy thought he must have fallen asleep. At last, with a *thrum*, the arrow flashed away. In the last light, it was barely visible as it streaked toward the target. Then there was a flash.

For one instant, Buddy could clearly see the painted

rectangle on the plywood. The arrow had struck the target just above the rectangle.

"Man, you can shoot apples off my head any time," Cool said.

"Just happen to have an apple in the bag," Rich said, beaming.

"Any time but now," Cool added.

"How about in the dark?" Buddy said. "How can you aim at something you can't see?"

"It's all worked out. I can see the window, right? That's what I aim at right now. But I've got the sights set so it'll hit high."

"For an M.R.," said Little Pie, "this kid shows a lot of class."

Everyone laughed except Buddy, who had an M.R. brother. He knew how people with good eyes made jokes about people who wore glasses, and how people who could hear well joked about "dummies" who could not. It was a sad fact of life. He seldom did anything about it unless someone, like that Cobra kid, called Ralphie Dum-Dum.

"When you thinking of doing this?" Cool asked.

"Anything wrong with tonight?" asked Rich.

"Now, wait a minute," Buddy said. "How are you going to shoot an arrow, then grab your camera and take a picture just when it hits?"

"Oh, man, you're so dumb! I'm going to set it for open flash, see? Means I focus the camera, and some-body else holds it with the shutter open. At night there isn't enough light to ruin the film. But when the flash goes off, that makes a picture. *Then* you close the shutter."

Traffic swooshed along overhead. They thought it over.

"Ol' Shriker," Rich said, "has prob'ly cooled off by now. And we don't even have to go inside the fence. So what can he do?"

Nothing, they decided. That huge and vicious man could do nothing. Nothing except mash them every way there was. . . .

13
Bull's-Eye!

In the dry and stifling weeds of the ridge, they lay waiting for the time to be right.

Not until dark had they gone up to the Atkins estate. One by one, like a combat team, they had entered the grove of old, dusty trees that stood like sentries around the building. They saw Shriker come out on the lawn in the moonlight and gaze around, much in the manner of a guard in a prison movie, the kind who was going to get grabbed from behind. But Shriker looked careless in the manner of a cat—slow and easy, but cocked, like a pistol.

Then he went inside. In a short time Buddy sniffed the odor of frying meat. He touched Little Pie's arm.

"He's cooking! Now's the time. He won't be watching."

Little Pie chewed his lips as though he were eating. It seemed to Buddy he was always nervous at night, perhaps a carryover from his days of combat with the Choppers.

"You know what's going to happen," he retorted in an angry whisper. "Somebody's going to sneeze, and that dude grabs us and we all go down to Eighty-seventh Street."

Eighty-seventh Street was the police station serving the Dogtown and Bandini Courts areas.

"If we're going to do it, this is the best time. If you're too chicken to do it, you can take off."

Little Pie gave Buddy a glare, got up, and walked to the fence.

"*Down!*" Cool hissed.

"He can't see us," said Little Pie calmly. "I can't hardly see the house, with all the shrubbery."

As they joined him, dead leaves as dry as paper crisped under their feet. Waves of gooseflesh raced over Buddy. He saw clearly the lights of the caretaker's cottage, but what Little Pie said was true: the shrubbery blocked everything out. The only place where there were no shrubs was at the gate. But no one wanted to stand there and be seen in the moonlight.

With Buddy carrying the bow, Cool the arrow, and Rich the camera, they sniffed around looking for a hole big enough to see the house and aim the camera. Buddy found a little alcove where the shrubs were less thick. Here a graveled path bordering the lawn swung up to a cement bench a foot inside the fence.

Buddy ducked down, squinting. In a half-squat, he could see Shriker moving back and forth between what were probably the stove and the table. But he could not see the window where the cat had lain. The bushes beside the fence were too thick. Sinking to his knees, he found he could just see the window. From this distance it was impossible to be sure whether the thing in the window was the cat or a sack of some kind.

He tiptoed along the fence and found Rich. "Take a look at this spot. I can see the window."

Rich went to his knees and squirmed around. "That's it, that's it! And I can set the camera on that bench . . ."

The lens was several times larger than the camera, like a fat telescope screwed into the front of it. Rich explained that it was a single-lens reflex camera; that meant that the telephoto lens was the same one you looked through to focus the camera. Passing the camera between the bars of the fence, he set it on the bench.

There was a fragrance of coffee. Buddy saw Shriker sit down to eat.

"String the bow for me," Rich muttered, while he made adjustments to the camera.

At last it was time to focus the lens. The bench, however, was too far inside the fence for Rich to get his eyes above the viewing screen. Carefully, he tried to ease his head between two of the black iron spears to get above the camera. The bars were too close to allow it.

"Gimme a hand," he whispered. "I'm sure it's that lousy cat, but I've got to focus sharp or we won't have anything. And all we're going to get is one shot."

"What do you want?"

"Two of you guys pull on these here bars. If you can give me a half-inch, I can get my head through."

Buddy and Cool set themselves, and pulled. The bars were thick and square, but they bent just enough to let Rich thrust his head through.

"Man," Cool breathed, "that ain't my idea of kicks!"

"One of you's going to have to do it, just the same," said Rich. "I'll be shooting the arrow."

"Double pay if Shriker catches us?" Buddy asked.

There were no volunteers, so they flipped a coin. Buddy lost. His stomach knotted up like a wet rope as he looked at Rich, trapped there. If Shriker came fast, he could cut his head off.

"There! Great! Let me out, now."

The boys again pulled at the bars and Rich drew his head out. Sitting on the bench, the camera was now aimed through the branches trailing across the path.

"Now, what you do," Rich told Buddy, "you push the trigger down *easy*. Wait 'til I say so—no use having it open any longer than we have to. And don't move the camera. Take your hands off it as soon as the shutter opens. When I see the flash, I'll close the shutter myself and take off with the camera. You other guys let him out, and we're home free."

Gripping an arm of each of the team supposed to release him, Buddy said: "You hear the man? Don't take off 'til I'm loose."

Little Pie chewed his lip like the last few morsels of a delicious dessert. Sweat glistened on him. He took hold of the bar; he and Cool let Buddy work his head through.

Rich moved along until he found a spot through which he could lob the arrow. He had Little Pie stand by with a second arrow in case the first missed fire. He said he could just about get two arrows off before Shriker realized what was going on. He locked the arrow to the bowstring, extended his arm, thrust the arrowpoint through the spears, and took long and careful aim.

"Open the shutter!" he whispered.

Buddy pressed the little chrome button on top of the camera. There was a greased *click*.

The arrow arched into the darkness with a fading *slip-slip-slip-slip*.

"Lemme out!" Buddy panted.

"Wait a minute—see if it—"

Crash!

Glass splintered in a chiming explosion. A cat uttered an angry yowl. A man bellowed something, and the kitchen light went out. The screen door banged open.

Rich reached down, pushed the trigger of the camera, and yanked it from the bench. "Man, oh, man!" he babbled. "Hit the window! Sounded like I might've hit the cat, too."

"Get me out!" Buddy chattered in panic.

The outside lights went on. Buddy made out the form of a man standing at a corner of the house holding a shotgun.

"Gotta take off with this camera!" Rich said. "I might have a picture. You guys help Buddy—"

Buddy tried to pull his head out, but his ears caught. He nearly tore them from his head pulling back.

"Come on, you idiots!" he pleaded. "Get me outa—"

Cool took hold of a bar. *Where the heck is Little Pie?* Buddy twisted his head. He heard people running, but Little Pie was gone.

"Come on, come on!" he begged.

"Man, I'm tryin'!"

A gun roared like a bull. Shotgun pellets tore the leaves to the left of the bench. Buddy sobbed with anxiety.

"Pull on them—please!"

"What the hell's going on out there? I'll blow you in two, whoever you are!" Shriker shouted.

He ran like a furious giant across the floodlit lawn toward them. Cool sobbed with exertion. Buddy reached up to help him, tried again to pull back. But it was a two-man job, and one of the men had deserted.

"Buddy, I got to take off!" Cool said. "Man, I'm sorry. I'll tell your folks. I got a rap sheet long as your arm, man, and I'd go back to placement for this—"

"No—please!" Buddy begged.

Shriker was moving swiftly toward them. He had heard their voices. He planted himself like Atlas supporting the world, and bawled:

"Speak up, now, or I'll blow you apart!"

Cool doubled over and ran. Buddy saw Shriker swivel the gun, trying to draw a bead on the sounds. If he fired, the pellets would go right into Buddy's face.

"Don't shoot!" he called. "I'm stuck in the fence."

He saw the caretaker hesitate, drop his head forward, and scrutinize the shrubbery. Then, step by step, the big man came toward the bench.

14
Wrecking Crew

When Shriker saw who it was, just a boy, he opened the gate and came around through the shrubbery to release him. Like a circus strong man, he simply took hold of the two bars and muscled them apart. Buddy ducked back and straightened up.

Shriker seized him by the neck with one hand. He held him at arm's-length, like a punching bag he was steadying before belting it. His fist was cocked. Close up, his features were battered; there were cuts in his eyebrows. Clearly, he had done some boxing before he became Miss Atkins's chauffeur.

"I told you kids," he said. "I warned you—"

"But we weren't on your property, Mr. Shriker," Buddy chattered.

"Just firing arrows at my property. Just trying to kill my cat."

"No, sir! We just—we—"

Shriker dragged him toward the gate. Still clutching him by the neck, he marched him to the house. He opened the screen door and shoved him inside, then touched a little red-eyed switch by the door. The red eye blinked out as the gate clanged in the night.

"You-all just what?" he demanded.

"Just wanted a picture of Buzzer."

"Why?"

"To see if—see if it was—"

"The same cat," said Shriker. "You miserable, low-lifing punks. So help me, if you've hurt that cat—"

He walked through the clean little parlor to the kitchen. Buddy followed him to the kitchen door and saw him pass through another door onto a back porch. A half-eaten plate of meat, potatoes, and peas lay on the table. A light was switched on. Shriker cursed. Out of sight he stormed around like a cyclone, then charged back into the kitchen to stare at Buddy.

"He's gone!"

Feeling dizzy and scooped out, Buddy asked, "Gone?"

"He jumped outa the window and taken off!"

"Gee, I'm sorry, Mr. Shriker! Maybe he's in another part of the house . . ."

Shriker, seizing him by the neck again, hauled him into the yard. They went to the broken window. It had an old-fashioned wooden sash, and the arrow had plowed right into the crossbar, a wooden plus sign, and smashed out three of the four panes. The battery on the arrow was still hanging on the wire. The flash cube was in place.

Shriker ripped the arrow from the sash and stared at it, then broke it in two and hurled the pieces across the floodlit lawn. "So help me! Get back in the house," he said.

Buddy hurried ahead of him. Shriker straight-armed

him into a chair. Then he dropped onto a green sofa and snatched a powder-blue telephone from an end table. He dialed a number and jammed the instrument against his ear.

In a moment he said, "Mrs. Podesta—this is Shriker. How are things, you say? Very bad, Mrs. Podesta. Very, *very* bad."

The phone crackled with excited female sounds. Shriker said:

"Well, if you'll turn it off for a minute, ma'am, I'll *tell* you what I mean. Those kids shot an arrow into the window, and Buzzer got away. —How do I know it was the kids?"

Shriker's gaze turned to Buddy. He smiled. Several of his teeth were off-color, and in an upper front tooth, gold-capped, a perfect star of sound tooth was revealed.

"I know because I'm looking at one of them right now," he stated. "I caught him, see? —Do that," he said. "I'll open the gate when you honk."

While they waited for the lady lawyer, he questioned Buddy.

Who told them to do it?

Did Buddy see the cat leave?

Was Hannibal messed up in this?

Far in the night, a siren wailed. Shriker's whole body pulled erect. He listened intently. Buddy listened, too. The siren sounds rose in volume.

Well, here it comes, he thought. *She's called the cops.*

". . . Listen here," Shriker said hastily. "I ain't laid a

hand on you, right? I had every legal right, but I didn't. Ain't that so?" He sounded anxious.

"Yes, sir. If it's the cops, I'll tell them the truth."

"The whole truth?"

Buddy sighed. "When they bring that wreckin' crew in on you," he said, "that's the kind you tell."

15
Scratch a Friend

It was Buddy's folks, not Mrs. Podesta, who had blown the whistle. Mr. and Mrs. Williams were waiting at the station when Buddy and Joel Shriker arrived in a squad car.

Upstairs in Juvenile Division, things looked like a block party.

Four of Buddy's friends were already being questioned on different matters. Soc Chavez had turned on all the fire hydrants along a busy street, causing a little foreign car to float a half-block before it made shore.

Rance Johnson had thrown a rock at some boys who had bad-mouthed him as they drove past, and a police car had accidentally taken the rock in the windshield.

Darnell Cooper had stolen a keg of beer off a truck.

Charles Grundy had dumped a can of detergent in the fountain at the Project office, and the Fire Department was still hosing away foam to uncover the building.

Fat Sergeant Swann took a phone call, and reported:

"Our gang liaison man says there's been a run on detergent at the stores, Captain! When these punks come up with the idea of dumping detergent in the street and *then* turning on the hydrants—"

The boys on the chairs brightened and sat up straighter. Captain Provo swatted the desk with his palm.

"For God's sake, Swann! Let them think up their own deviltry, will you? The Department's crime graph is going to bust us all to patrolman next month as it is! Look at that curve!"

He indicated a chart on a wall. Buddy saw a graph that looked like the life span of Average Male Cat at the club. From a steady little seesaw of misdemeanors, the curve had taken a strong and wicked climb toward total delinquency, just on the day the club had closed.

They couldn't say Mr. Hannibal hadn't warned them.

The captain squared off to Shriker as he and Buddy were led forward. Shriker wore the full-dress uniform of his own design—black boots, pale-blue trousers and tunic, and a black shirt and cap.

"Now, what?" the captain said.

Shriker explained his side of the affair. Buddy realized that Shriker was in the position of any Negro in any police station: restless, ill-at-ease, under an invisible thumb. Though he was the complaining witness, he came from a long line of people whose experiences with the law had been universally bad. He began sounding as though the next thing he would say was: *Oh, well, forget it.*

On a scarred bench against the wall, Buddy's parents listened. Mrs. Williams's eyes were closed, and she hummed a hymn. But Buddy's father was on his toes, weighing everything Shriker said like a diamond merchant with his tiny scales.

Gonna need all the leverage we can get, his expression said.

One night, when Buddy was twelve and had been very bad, and everybody was sick, and his father was just getting over the flu, Mr. Williams had openhanded him in such a way that Buddy flew across a bed and hit the wall.

There was a feeling in Buddy that this was going to be one of those nights.

"Do you want to make a statement?" the captain asked Buddy.

"Yes, sir. I didn't do it," Buddy said.

"Didn't do what?"

"Shoot that arrow."

"But you were there?"

"Yes, sir. Just watching, though. Didn't trespass or anything, Captain."

A police officer opened the door. "A lady would like—" he began.

Mrs. Podesta came in. She smiled at everyone, especially Buddy. Then she sat down by the Williamses.

"I'm an attorney, Captain," she said. "I represent Mr. Shriker and Buddy Williams."

"Both of them?" The captain rolled a newspaper like a club. "That's illegal, lady. What's your name?"

Mrs. Podesta told him who she was, while she drew from a tapestry bag a wad of knitting with amber needles thrust into it. As she talked, she dumped balls of yarn on the floor and began clattering the needles.

"Lady—" began the captain.

"At any rate," said Mrs. Podesta, her sunken eyes serene in her skull, "I represent Mr. Shriker and I offer the boy free advice. Tell the truth, darling, and no one can touch you." She smiled at Buddy. "Have you told the truth?"

"Yes, ma'am," Buddy said.

"You see?" she said happily. "Now, Joel, you aren't going to run the risk of a terrible lawsuit for false arrest by signing a complaint against Buddy on no evidence at all, are you? Considering that you can't prove a thing?"

It stopped Shriker like a swing to the chin. He scowled like a caveman trying to understand algebra. He did not get it at all. Wasn't this his lawyer? He looked around at the policemen, puzzled. Buddy thought of a battered old fighter who didn't know whom to hit.

"All I know," he said, "is I lost a window, and my cat's gone."

"Insurance will repair the window, and we'll find the cat."

"How you going to do that, ma'am?" asked Shriker.

"I telephoned the newspapers before I came down. We're offering a reward of five hundred dollars for the return of Buzzer."

Among the boys waiting to be charged for their various offenses, a mutter arose as though a bell had just rung for recess. Five hundred dollars! Buddy could already picture people swarming up and down alleys and over fences. For five hundred dollars, Dogtown would have searched a mile of junkyards for a lost valve cap.

"Does that include policemen?" asked Sergeant Swann quickly.

Mrs. Podesta gave him her mad smile. "Policemen *especially*," she replied. "Boys," she said to the group waiting to be formally charged, "what are you all here for?"

They told her. In the end, Mrs. Podesta got everybody sprung, on bail or otherwise.

Captain Provo seemed actually grateful. He confided to Buddy's father.

"If it wasn't for that reward, this town would be up to its eyeballs in soapsuds before midnight! If the budget will afford it, I'm going to keep a cat hunt going all summer."

Mrs. Podesta, stuffing five pounds of yarn into a two-pound bag, asked Mrs. Williams if she might visit their home for a few minutes.

"We'd be pleased," said Mrs. Williams, puzzled.

Buddy had an anxious feeling about the woman, as though if she picked enough of their hairs off the couch she would have a whole squad of voodoo workers casting spells on them tomorrow. . . .

"What a lovely little home!" cried Mrs. Podesta. She had carried a photograph album and a small tape recorder up from the car.

"Thank you," said Mrs. Williams. "Tom and I—"

"Do you like dogs?" Mrs. Podesta asked the family.

"I like dogs!" said Ralphie. Wearing pajamas, he had slipped in unseen.

"Oh, how sweet!" said Mrs. Podesta. She patted Ralphie on the head. "I brought some pictures of *my* boys for you to look at. And when you turn on the tape recorder—like this"—she pressed a switch—"you can hear them as well as see them!"

The room was filled with the snarling and yapping of a kennel full of hungry hounds. Mrs. Podesta's voice could be heard under the uproar, saying, "Boys, be good," and, "Rex, stop that!" and such things. Eagerly, Ralphie began turning pages in the album. Buddy watched Mrs. Podesta move toward the door to the kitchen, smiling emptily.

Buddy's parents seemed nonplused. How do you entertain a nut? was the problem.

But Mrs. Podesta entertained herself, drifting through the house, speaking to Angie or to Mrs. Williams, saying how cute this and that was. She exclaimed over the wigs sitting on Angie's dresser on styrofoam Beethovens. The jar of soap buds in the bathroom was precious, she thought. And Buddy's room was so *typically* a boy's room, she said, as she pulled the landing gear of a low-hung model airplane out of her hair.

The point was, Buddy suddenly realized, to get into every room of the house as fast as possible.

She was looking for Buzzer.

Tight-lipped, she returned at last to the parlor. Then her crazy smile flashed, and she sat beside Ralphie. The roar of hounds filled the parlor.

"Shall we turn the player off now, dear?" she said, as though turning it on had been his idea.

Mrs. Williams offered a cup of coffee. It was past eleven, and people were beginning to look sleepy.

"No, I mustn't stay," said Mrs. Podesta. "May I speak very frankly? Mr. Shriker loves that cat very, very much. Just as though it were a child."

"It supports him," said Mr. Williams pleasantly. "I guess he should love it."

"He'll move heaven and earth to recover Buzzer Atkins," declared Mrs. Podesta.

"So will we," said Mrs. Williams. "Buddy is very sorry he played a part in the cat's getting loose."

"I'm sure he is," agreed the lawyer woman. "In the event that the cat isn't found, I know he'll be even sorrier. It's just as easy to make the law work one way as another. Tonight I wanted it to work toward getting Buddy out, so he could tell me where the cat is. But he hasn't told me. Later, I might want it to work the other way."

"I'm not sure I understand," said Mr. Williams coldly.

Mrs. Podesta got up. Again she was smiling. "Oh, I think we all understand one another," she said. "Good night. Such a nice home. A comfortable bed for everyone, too."

They heard her gun her car away from the curb, burning rubber. Fiercely she cornered toward Ajax Street. She was giving the car the beating, Buddy realized, that she could not give him.

"It's hard to be sure," said Mr. Williams, "but I think what she just said was that if Buddy doesn't come up with the cat, she'll do all she can to get him jailed."

"I didn't do anything," Buddy said. "Nothing real bad."

His nostrils flaring, his father said: "Trespassing, even with part of your body only, is a misdemeanor. Aiding and abetting vandalism is a misdemeanor, too. But *conspiring* with others to commit a misdemeanor happens to be a felony! A smart prosecutor who wanted to give you a hard time could do it. You're right next door to doing time, young fellow!"

Just before Buddy climbed in bed, the telephone rang. Mr. Williams answered it, then called Buddy.

"This is Pastelito," the caller said.

"Uh-huh," Buddy said coolly. "Hah you, man?"

"*Ah-see, ah-see*," said Little Pie, in Spanish, meaning, *So-so*. "You okay?" he asked.

"Uh-huh."

"Listen. I wanted to tell you why I cut out tonight."

"I was wondering."

"I'm on probation for a Nark rap, that's why. I couldn't afford to get caught."

"Tough."

"It was one of those stupid things, you know? A party

I was at couple of years ago where they were smoking grass. I might have taken a couple of drags, no more. I don't need that stuff. I mean, you know, things are tough enough without a habit, right?"

"Right."

"But I got busted for just being there. I pulled three years' probation. So if I got picked up tonight, I'd be looking down the barrel of that old rap, too."

"I know how it is. I'm hoping probation's all I get. My father says I could get a felony rap for this. Conspiracy or something."

"Chihuahua!" Little Pie groaned. "He's just trying to scare you, huh?"

"No, Mrs. Podesta threatened to get me, too."

The line hummed. "If it would help, I'd go to the fuzz and tell them I was there," Little Pie said.

"No, no. You played it just right. If you'd hung around, you mighta got caught. This way I can take the rap for the whole gang, see? You played it real smart. So long, bean. *Nos huachamos*, huh?"

Scratch one friend, thought Buddy. *When you really need him, he isn't there.*

16
Ding, Dong, Bell!

Mr. Williams had left early to catch a parolee who lived across town before he went to work. Mrs. Williams had already left for the service center where she worked. Angie cooked breakfast. A warm breeze puffed up the lace curtains of the kitchenette window like balloons. Ralphie pushed his finger into a swelling curtain, trying to make it pop.

Before he got up, Buddy had heard Angie talking on the telephone to half the girls in Dogtown.

"I can find him! I know I can!" she told everyone. Cats like me—I'm the Pied Piperette of Dogtown. I'm going to spend a hundred dollars of the reward money on clothes, and put the rest in the bank toward a piano—"

". . . Oh, man! you've got to be out of your mind," Buddy said, as they ate. "I saw at least twenty guys climb the back fence this morning to see if the cat was in the yard! And one of them was over fifty years old. Everybody that can walk is out hunting Buzzer."

"Including me."

Angie's eyes danced. But she also wore an expression of sorrow and kindliness, like Florence Nightingale or someone. "Poor thing! He'll be so scared that he'll be hiding somewhere. He's never been out where there were dogs and boys before."

Buddy snorted. "How come he's going to come out of hiding for you?"

"Because I'm going to be dangling a little piece of ribbon. Cats love to chase ribbons. And I'll have a basket to pop him into—"

"You keep talking wild, Angie, and somebody's going to pop you into a basket. Twenty-year-old cats don't chase ribbons—only young ones."

"If it's the same Buzzer Miss Atkins left the money to, then I don't want him. I'd rather he stayed lost. But if it's a young cat, I want him, so we can shame Shriker. I'll keep him, too."

Buddy blinked. This kid was not so dumb, at that. Only when she talked to her friends on the telephone.

"You wants me to go with you," Ralphie said to Angie.

"Sure, honey. Brush your teeth *real good*, now."

"Ding, dong, bell!" Ralphie cried, jumping up.

"Don't forget to check all the old wells," Buddy called to Angie as she left the kitchen.

He propped his head in his hands and stared out the window. Four boys were coming up the street, glancing into every yard and alley and under porches. They were all strangers to him. He was thinking that however things went, now, his tail was caught in a crack. If the cat were found, and it was not the real Buzzer, then Mrs.

Podesta would get revenge by going after Buddy Williams. She was a lawyer, and she knew how to make trouble.

If it turned out to be the original—the one and only Buzzer Atkins of the newspaper picture—then the Boys Club lost out. A cat that could live twenty-odd years might live forty, with the kind of care Buzzer was getting.

About eleven, Buddy heard the croupy sound of Cool's auto horn up the street. He went out onto the roof of the garage. As he watched Cool moor the old dreadnaught at the curb, its front bumper hanging low on the right, like the horn of a battered bull, he noticed a car parked across the street. A man sat at the wheel reading a newspaper.

The man glanced at Cool, then back at the newspaper. There was nothing unusual about the man, except that he did not belong in the neighborhood. Cool untwisted the wire that held the driver's door closed, got out, and trotted up the steps.

"Hear about Rich?" Cool asked, sitting down in the shade. He tossed up an iron pill and caught it in his mouth.

Buddy jumped. Cool had a way of saying it was going to rain today that made it sound like you'd better start getting bids on your ark.

"No! What happened to him?" Buddy asked.

"Nothing. I mean he got permission to use a darkroom at the newspaper office. He took the bus down this morning, and he'll prolly be back by five," he said.

"Five! How many pictures is he going to print, for Pete's sake?"

"Just one—if we got one. But it's a couple hours on the bus, and he's got to wait for when they aren't using the darkroom."

"That'll be about Sunday," Buddy predicted.

The telephone rang. It was Mrs. Podesta.

"Have you decided to tell the truth about Buzzer?" she cried. She sounded wild.

"I don't know anything about him," Buddy said.

"Then you're the only person in the city who doesn't," snapped the woman. "I'm out of my mind with people wanting to sell me a cat for five hundred dollars."

As Buddy walked out again, Cool was saying, "There come your sister and Ralphie."

Buddy hurried to the edge of the porch and gazed down the street. Angie was sauntering along as though nothing in life were important enough to push her into a fast trot. But everybody had a special way of walking; and the way Angie was walking was not hers. She had something in the basket! Just then Ralphie saw Buddy, and he began waving excitedly. Angie seized his arm and he stared down at the sidewalk and stopped waving.

"She's got something!" Buddy said to Cool.

He looked at the man parked across the street. He had been sitting there so long the top of his car was littered with pepper-tree leaves. And still he was reading the newspaper! Something wrong with that man. Was he a bill collector? A plainclothesman?"

"See that cat down there?" he muttered to Cool.

Cool took off his heavy black-framed glasses, and squinted.

"Looks like— Yeah, I think it is! That's Sergeant Bibbs. He works Nark. *Think* that's him—"

Buddy shivered.

Had Mrs. Podesta sicced the narcotics squad on him, now? Would they be tearing his mattress apart looking for little capsules?

Climbing slowly, Angie and Ralphie reached the porch. Then Buddy saw his sister's eyes! They gleamed like an animal's eyes when headlights struck them at night. Her hands were clenched around the handle of the picnic basket as though it weighed a hundred pounds.

"We've got him!" she whispered. "We've got Buzzer!"

17
Buzzer Number Two

Angie set the picnic basket on the parlor table. Then she leaned down and said:

"Honey? We're going to let you out, now. Isn't that nice?"

"Well, let him out!" Cool hissed.

Angie unhooked the clasp and raised the lid a few inches. A black paw appeared. A cat yowled. Then a white paw came in view, and a white nose. Like a gymnast chinning himself, a cat pulled his head and shoulders clear of the basket and gazed at them with big yellow eyes.

"Quick! Get the picture!" Angie whispered.

Buddy darted to the kitchen drawer where they had stored the picture of Shriker holding Miss Atkins's cats —the print of the old newspaper picture. *Black right ear—white left. Was that it? No—white right ear, wasn't it?*

He yanked the drawer open. From a drift of cookbooks and recipes torn from magazines, he drew the shiny eight-by-ten print of the old newspaper photo. He stared at it and gave a yelp.

"Black right ear!" he cried.

"Black *left* ear!" Cool shouted. "This here's a different cat."

Anxiety bore Buddy down like a ton of ice cubes.

"But how do we know it's Shriker's cat?" he said in a moment, afraid to hope that Shriker was caught in the crime of the century.

"I'll show how we know—"

Angie picked up the big soft tomcat and cuddled him. From the thick fur of his throat, she lifted a tiny gold medallion on a chain. Turning it over, she read:

" 'My name is Buzzer Atkins. If found, please return me to J. Shriker, 110 Hilltop Road. Big Reward.' "

". . . Well, now, look!" Cool pulled his fish knife out of his pocket and gestured with it as he tried to understand. "If that ain't the same cat as the one in the picture, then Buzzer Atkins is dead! Ain't that so?"

"That is so." Bubbles sparkled up through Buddy like those in a bottle of soda water. "And this nice kitty-cat is a stand-in. He isn't any more Buzzer Atkins than we are. We've got Shriker and that woman in the corner!"

". . . 'Scuse me, young people," said a polite voice.

All of them turned, startled. In the doorway stood a neatly dressed Negro in a dark business suit. He was wearing tan leather gloves and carrying a portable pet cage. Aside from the glasses, he looked like a social worker. He drew a wallet from his pocket and flipped it open, smiling.

"Lieutenant Gshmortz," he said. "I have a warrant for this cat." Placing the pet cage on the table, he took the cat from Angie's arms. "Now, ain't he a cute little feller?"

"Wait a minute. You've been parked across the street, haven't you?" Buddy asked him.

"That is correct, lad," said the man. "I thought, What's the use plodding all over town, when the kids that stole the cat will bring him back here sooner or later anyway?"

"We didn't steal him!" Angie retorted. "My brother and I found him not a block from where he lives. I knew he'd stay close to home. He was chasing birds in the brush. But he's so out of condition from being locked up that he couldn't catch his tail."

Raising a hinged trapdoor in the cage, the man lowered Buzzer into it and snapped it closed.

"There, now! On the way to the rightful owner. For an old cat, he's right spry. Been real nice knowing you, folks. Take care now."

Like that he was gone.

The screen door closed quietly behind him.

"You can't just go busting in somebody's house like— like—" Buddy protested to Angie and Cool.

"He did. Said something about a warrant, didn't he?" Cool recalled. "I ain't messing around with no law—"

"What was his name?" Angie frowned. "Lieutenant Schwartz? Schmortz?"

"Get his license number!" Buddy blurted. He ran for the porch.

They ran to the edge of the garage roof. A car engine started. Cool put his hands to his mouth, and bawled:

"We'll turn you in! There's a reward for that cat!"

Buddy arrived as, waving, the man drove off. Buddy shouted in anger. He threw a small stone after the car, the only one he could find. Then he faced the others furiously.

"What's the matter with us? That was Lieutenant Nobody—just a private eye that woman put on us."

"Somebody owes us $500," Cool said, "whichever tomcat it was Angie's caught."

Heartbrokenly, Angie dropped onto a bench. "That was the sweetest old cat I ever held. And you know, he wasn't so old. His fur was just as soft, and his teeth were white, and—"

"Did he have a false tooth?" Buddy asked.

"Yes. I could see it just as plain. There were little gold wires fastening it to the teeth alongside. Isn't that right, Ralphie?"

Ralphie, spooning green Jell-O from a box, muttered: " 'Please return me to 110 Hilltop Road—' "

"*Didn't* he have a false tooth?" Angie asked.

"He had a false tooth, Angie," Ralphie said.

"*Sounds* like it was the same cat that got left the money, then," Buddy frowned.

"But look, man," Cool argued, "if it is, he's had an ear job. Because they're on the wrong sides of his head."

"Better call Mr. Hannibal," Buddy decided.

Buddy went into the house and dialed Mr. Hannibal's number. But though he let the telephone ring and ring, no one answered. He went back to the porch. "Nobody home."

"Somebody coming," Cool said, peering toward the street.

Rich came into view at the top of the steps. In one hand he carried a large brown envelope. Angie ran to him.

"We had him, Rich, we had him!" she wailed. "I had him right in my arms!"

Rich slumped into a chair and tossed the envelope on the table. "Who? Shriker?"

"Buzzer! I caught him near his house. He had a little medal that said, 'My name is Buzzer Atkins.' But it wasn't the real Buzzer at all. The ears were wrong."

"And some private-eye dude just walked right in and grabbed him," Cool said.

Still breathing hard from the climb, Rich looked at each in turn. "Sometimes I wonder about you cats," he said. "I don't think you even know which side the black ear's supposed to be on."

"The right side!" they said. At last everyone had it down pat.

Rich rubbed his neck. "No, no. You're right about the black ear, but wrong about the cat. It's Buzzer, all right. Look at the picture we got."

He drew some prints from the envelope; they were still slightly damp. They crowded around to look. Even Ralphie was curious.

Buzzer had heard the arrow before it struck. His head was tilted and he was making a savage spitting-cat face. Fragments of glass shone on his coat and lay gleaming in the folds of a crumpled paper sack lying on the window ledge. The face of a cat could be seen on the sack. The sack had held pet food.

The flashbulb had exploded a foot from Buzzer, and every whisker showed, every claw, every tooth. Even the false tooth, one of the long upper teeth, was revealed in his snarl. In his neck hairs shone the little gold medallion.

Buddy's stomach dropped as he compared the ears in the two prints. They were identical. Black right ear, white left.

Buzzer Atkins lived!

Ralphie, who could not have understood, not knowing right from left, seemed oddly disturbed. His lower lip quivering, he pointed at the new picture.

"That is doof God deena tack," he said.

"What, honey?" Angie said.

"Doof God deena tack. I don't like doof God!"

"Oh, man," Buddy moaned. When Ralphie got hung up on something, it could go on for days. Photos often threw him. He had a strange way of scratching his own image off any family picture he saw. Buddy hoped this wasn't the start of a long hang-up.

"I don't know what you mean, honey," Angie told Ralphie.

Ralphie made a grab for the picture, but Buddy pulled it away just in time.

"That is doof God—!" Ralphie wailed, as Angie said sharply:

"Don't say God unless you're praying."

"I'm praying, I'm praying!" Buddy groaned. He gazed sadly at Rich. "We just lost a half-million bucks on your photography, you hot-dog photog."

Cool might be slow at some things, but facts stuck in his mind like foxtails in a sock.

"Well, man—man, look. What I mean, we were *lookin'* at that cat!" he said. "And that ain't the way he was wearing his ears today. So there's got to be two cats."

"Each wearing a medal?" Rich said. "And each with a little fleck by his nose? Or didn't the cat you saw have that little black fleck on his nose?"

"Yes!" Angie said. "I can still see it, just as plain—"

"But he was wearing his ears different," Rich scoffed.

"Maybe he's got ear wigs," Buddy said to Angie, "like you got hair wigs, and he changes them according to what tabby cat he's going out with."

Ralphie was crying quietly. When Angie looked at him, he pointed at the envelope and said again:

"That is doof God—"

"Don't know about alla you," Cool said, hitching up his pants, "but I'm going down to González Grocery and hook a couple of six-packs out of the back room as soon as it's dark. Anybody care to be my guest?"

Buddy said disgustedly: "No, I'll just stay home and pray to doof God. Oh, man! The long hot summer . . ."

18
The Bad List

At last the great cat hunt was over.

It had come to a bewildering end, like a chase in the Hall of Mirrors. How many Buzzers were there? Was Buzzer only a ghost that lay in the window at night?

For how could there possibly be two cats with absolutely identical markings—even to a false tooth—but with the ears reversed?

Angie was furious about losing the cat and the reward both. She was getting ready to visit the police station to swear out a warrant for the private detective's arrest when her mother stopped her.

"And what do you think would happen to Buddy?" she asked. "Mrs. Podesta would have him back in hot water in no time."

"Well, I wish I had Buzzer. I'd almost as soon have him as the money. Almost. You know, he really *talked* to me!"

Oh, my aching bank account! Buddy thought, lying on the living room floor, drinking a Coke while Angie and her mother talked in the kitchen. *As soon have a cat as five hundred dollars!* Angie was ironing while her mother made another pie. She was pie-happy these days.

The strategy seemed to be that if she stuffed enough pastry into Buddy and his friends, they would be too fat and lazy to get into any more trouble. Fat people did get into less trouble, at that. Kinda seemed that way. His thoughts were shuffling down this pointless dead end when the telephone rang.

"One, two, three, four, guess who that's for?" Ralphie chanted, licking a Jell-O wrapper.

". . . Why, surely," Buddy heard his mother saying. "I know he'd be just delighted. A going-away affair? Oh, no! You can't mean—"

Buddy sat up, poker-faced but shocked.

"Who's going where?" he asked when his mother came into the parlor.

"You and Ralph are going over to the Hannibals' home for a paint-in," she said. "There'll be brushes and food for everybody. They're asking about six boys to help them paint the house."

"How come?"

His mother sighed. "Mr. Hannibal had to accept that job in Cleveland. They're getting the house ready to sell, and they thought you might like to help out by doing some painting. . . ."

Ralphie and Buddy were the first to arrive. The Hannibals lived across the street from Memorial High, in a small white bungalow with green trim and a twisted cedar in the yard like a stunted Japanese tree in a dish. A picket fence enclosed the tiny lawn. Beside the front steps stood twin bushes with little flowers that looked like dancers with red tops and flaring white skirts.

Next door, a woman in a bathrobe was sweeping the walk in a slow motion. Buddy saw her lean down and pick a few weeds, then sweep some more. *Swish, swish, swish*. Just killing time; chopping it up like kindling. Which was what half the people in Dogtown did. No job, no car, no club. Yet a good man like Mr. Hannibal, who made things run the way gasoline ran a car, had to leave town to find work.

Through Buddy there ran a confused anger at nothing specific but everything in general.

Mrs. Hannibal, a tall woman with dark rosewood skin and warm brown eyes, let them in. Ralphie saw the three slim gold bracelets on her wrist, and had to touch them. She showed him how they were linked together. Then he discovered the portable typewriter on a card table, and yelled:

" *'List A: Contributing Members! Alcorn, Howard—'* "

"That's right, honey," Mrs. Hannibal said. "Do you know the terrible thing that happened when the Boys Club blew up? All our records were destroyed! Hundreds and hundreds of names—"

Her glance went to Buddy. "Do you think there's any chance that Ralphie can remember most of the membership list? Even though there is no club at the moment, there will be, and whoever takes Lloyd's place will need to notify the boys when the club reopens."

"Remember? Like he can't forget, Mrs. Hannibal!"

Already uncovering the machine, Ralphie cried out in excitement: "Which list? Which list?"

"List C, isn't it? Members in good standing."

"List D—List D!" said Ralphie. Beside the machine were stacked a half-dozen packets of three-by-five cards. Rolling the first card into the typewriter, Ralphie chattered a name and address and began typing.

"It's just fantastic," Mrs. Hannibal exclaimed. "Do you really think he can—"

Buddy tapped his head. "He's got it up here. The human computer. He'll do until filing systems are invented."

Mrs. Hannibal shook her head in wonder. "Lloyd's out back mixing paint," she said. "The other boys will be along soon."

Little Pie was the second boy to arrive. Buddy gave him the cold eye and said nothing in reply to his greeting.

"Rich showed me the pictures," Mr. Hannibal told them. There were flecks of white paint in his short spadelike beard. "The ears were certainly the same in both the old newspaper photo and the one you boys took. But the rest of the older picture was too blurred to tell much."

Buddy got edgy when he even thought about the cat. It was like having a tune run through your head until you were sick of it; yet you could not turn it off. Everything about the cat had been hard luck for him. The matter was settled of whether Buzzer Atkins lived. But at the core of it all there still lay a mystery he could not fathom.

". . . Wish I'd been there when Angie brought that cat in," Little Pie was saying. "I got this photographic memory. I could close my eyes and tell you exac'ly how he was wearing his ears—"

He closed his eyes and waved the paintbrush mysteriously to demonstrate how his memory worked.

"A little to the right," Buddy said, "and you'll have a white ear like Buzzer."

"There has got," said the director, "to be something funny going on up there. If a cat can switch ears between the time you take his picture and develop it, then he's the most remarkable feline in history. Same cat, right down to flecks, and the tag around his neck—but when you take his picture his ears cross over. Do you believe that?"

"No."

"Neither do I."

The back door opened and three more boys arrived: Soc Chavez, Charles Grundy, and Rance Johnson. That left only Darnell Cooper, of the most likely troublemakers in the club. Mr. Hannibal knew which boys to pull off the streets when he could. He gave them brushes and rollers and showed each where to paint.

"After a while," he said, "we'll have hot dogs and something to drink."

Buddy had smelled Rance's breath and knew he had

already had something to drink. But he was painting pretty steady even so.

As obsessed with cats as Ralphie was with Jell-O, Mr. Hannibal hauled back to Buzzer once more.

"I came across the bill for Buzzer's bridge while I was filing some things. It was put in only two months ago."

"What's a bridge?" asked Little Pie.

"A false tooth. Now, that could mean one of two things. Either the old bridge fell out and had to be replaced, as Mrs. Podesta claims. Or . . ."

Paintbrush upraised, he went silent, commanding their attention. All heads turned. Little Pie had paint all over his face already. Buddy had a swatch across his throat like a wound. Mr. Hannibal's voice dropped almost to a whisper.

"Or," he continued, "Buzzer Atkins died two months ago, and they installed a false tooth in the head of his replacement!"

His breath catching in his throat, Buddy said: "That's got to be it! Because that was a young tomcat Angie brought home. He was no twenty years old, I'll guaran-darn-tee you."

"Did you ask the vet about it?" Little Pie asked.

"Yes, but that man's making hundreds of dollars a year taking care of the cat, so you know who's side *he's* on. He said it was the same cat."

Suddenly Buddy shivered.

It was like being alone in the house at night, and all at once you felt a draft, and knew a door had been opened; or you smelled tobacco smoke . . .

He had remembered something. And tied onto that memory, like the tail of a kite, was a fact so simple and terrible that his mind raced away from it in fear.

"—Well, if the old cat died," Little Pie was saying, "they musta buried him someplace, huh?"

"I suppose. They wouldn't dare just throw him out in the brush like a lot of folks would. Or bury him where he might accidentally be dug up by an animal—"

Little Pie's mouth fell open. He looked at Buddy. He was going to yell it out, the thing they had both remembered. But Buddy scowled him to silence.

Hastily they both went back to painting.

Five minutes later, Mr. Hannibal said, "I'd better see how Ralph's doing."

"Mr. Hannibal!" Buddy blurted.

Surprised, the director turned back. "Yes?"

"You're really going to leave Dogtown, huh?"

"Have to, boy. I could get a loan and hang on till fall, but there's no point in it now. And if I put it off any longer, they won't hold that job for me."

Wiping his hands on a paint rag, he went into the house.

So, Buddy knew, it had come to the point he had feared. All or nothing. For he and Little Pie knew where the body was buried, and one of them was going to have to dig it up tonight.

19
The Strongbox

In silence, they continued to paint. As he sliced excess paint from the edge of his brush on a tray, Buddy said under his breath:

"You know where he's buried, don't you?"

"Sure. Under Buzzer's window."

"Where the dog was digging that night when Shriker threw a rock at him. And when I was stuck in the fence—did you see him charge out and look there first?"

"No, I was—you know—" Little Pie hesitated.

"You were running too fast," Buddy said.

With one finger, Little Pie tried to work out a fly that had got stuck in the painted wall. "I hit the panic button that time," he admitted. "Won't happen again."

"Better not, 'cause this time you'll be the one digging up the body. It's my turn to watch."

Little Pie had the fly off the wall, but now he could not get it off his finger. He shook it, saying:

"Whatcha think about telling Mr. Hannibal? And maybe he can get a paper from the Court to let us dig him up?"

"Whatcha think Shriker's going to be doing while we try to get that paper? He'll be digging up the body and moving it, that's what."

136

The fly whipped off Little Pie's finger, but landed in the paint again. Scowling, he painted right over it.

"That's a fact," he said.

"And we haven't got much time."

"You talking about tonight?" Little Pie sounded uneasy.

"Tell me a better time."

"Just me and you?"

"No use taking a whole mob up there."

Little Pie gnawed on a knuckle. "Man, I wouldn't have a prayer! Diggin' right under that window? And how do I get over the fence?"

"Still some details to work out," said Buddy light-heartedly.

They smelled wieners frying, and soon Mrs. Hannibal called to them to clean up. The back of the house had been painted, and the rest of it could be finished before sundown. They ate, then resumed work. From the house came the steady clatter of the typewriter. Mrs. Hannibal reported that Ralphie had finished List D and was starting on List A.

Dusk burned in the sky like the smoke of a trash fire. With the work finished, the other boys left, flexing sore shoulders and stiff necks. Little Pie had said he would meet Buddy at Crabby Mike's Pizza Stand at eight o'clock. Ralphie began to cry when they said he had to quit, now. So Mrs. Hannibal called Mrs. Williams.

"—He's having *such* a good time, and he's no trouble at all. Just the best boy there ever was."

Ralphie bounced up and down and repeated her words to Buddy. Buddy patted his head.

"—He can have dinner with us, and when he's tired Lloyd will take him home."

"Won't you eat with us too?" Mrs. Hannibal asked Buddy, after she had hung up.

"No, thanks. My father's going to give me a driving lesson tonight."

"Fine, then."

Mr. Hannibal walked him to the front. He tried to sound hearty when he thanked Buddy for his help, but sorrow rang in his voice.

"I'm going to miss you fellows. You've been like our own kids since our girls married."

"We'll be seeing you again, Mr. Hannibal," Buddy said.

"Of course," said Mr. Hannibal. He spoke curtly, as though suddenly angry. Buddy suspected that he was afraid his voice would break. For the first time, he knew how much the club had meant to Mr. Hannibal, who had built it the way a preacher might build his church. And now they would no longer let him preach in it.

Buddy called his home from the pizza stand on Ajax Street.

"—It's all done. Cool's going to give me a driving lesson. My learner's permit's still good. I'll be home about nine."

At a picnic table, Buddy and Little Pie ate pizza from waxed papers. Traffic clattered by. The jukebox loudspeaker brayed over these sounds. Next door, littered with broken bottles, was the concrete foundation of a store long since demolished. Near the sidewalk was a huge pile of trash awaiting pickup. It had been there for weeks. This was Do-It-Yourselfville, as far as the city was concerned, and ten years from now, he knew, the Boys Club would be the same pile of junk it was—unless they succeeded in shaking Mrs. Podesta and Shriker loose from that money.

Little Pie took an ice cube from his drink. He passed it back and forth from one hand to the other.

"I got it psyched out how I'm going over the fence," he said.

Buddy hunched forward, smiling. "Tell me, man."

"I'm going over the gate—the only place where there isn't shrubbery to get tangled in. There's no moon tonight, and unless he turns on the floodlights, it'll be pitch-dark there."

"Got it psyched out where you'll get a ladder?"

"From one of the houses along Lopez Street. You know those little busted picket fences? One of those."

Buddy pictured the broken fences along the narrow side-hill street. Nearly every house had a remnant of a fence—two long runners with slats for pickets. Half the slats were missing, but they would need a piece only six or eight feet long.

"Let's see, now," he said, starting to fold his pizza paper into a glider. "You go up and jump down onto the drive, right? Then how do you get back?"

"As soon as I go over, I head for the house. While I'm

gone, you slide the ladder under the gate. I'll pick it up when I get back."

"What're you going to dig with?"

Little Pie opened his shirt. He pulled an orange-handled trowel into view. "I borrowed this from the Hannibals. Don't think they'll mind. . . ."

Buddy sailed the glider into a trash barrel, and they left.

In the warm evening, Lopez Street was like a jungle trail, with tropical plants gone wild, a softness in the air, and the fragrances of night-blooming blossoms. He sniffed. Someone was barbecuing spareribs over a hole in his backyard. Edging into the dirt street were trash barrels and overgrown geraniums. In a front-yard container of old tires stacked like doughnuts, someone had planted a camellia bush.

With his elbow, Little Pie alerted Buddy.

Just ahead, on the right, stood a little picket fence. They made sure no one was on the porch, then checked it out. But it was too puny—merely rusty nails and rotten wood.

Farther along was another fence—just right, except that it was too sound to remove without an uproar.

They walked on, two figures in paint-splashed jeans, tennis shoes and T-shirts. They moved silently, haunting the smoky byways of Upper Dogtown. In a house, a child cried and a man spoke sharply to it in Spanish. A radio played in a bedroom, and they watched, for a moment, the silhouette of a girl dancing by herself. Buddy sighed.

Leaning down, he tugged at a crooked fence. This was the one! Sound enough, but not too sound, and unpainted so that it would not reveal itself. Grasping a slat, he pulled on it. The stake slipped from the ground.

In silence, they set to work removing a section of the fence. It was so overhung by dusty geraniums that it almost required a gardener to free the fence.

At last it came up—seven feet long, a foot and a half wide. Carrying it like Little League firemen, they headed for Hilltop Drive.

20
Trapped!

For fifteen minutes they lay in the weeds beside Shriker's driveway. The night opened to Buddy's senses like a flower. His eyes searched the gate. He studied the dense shrubbery. The little house gave off, even at this distance, an aroma of steak. His mouth watered. That evil man—living on steak when honest people were trying to stretch a stewing hen through Sunday dinner, chicken salad, and decent burial in a graveyard of noodles.

He searched the heavy swatches of shrubbery inside the fence. It might be Shriker's style to cook a steak for bait, and post himself outside with a shotgun.

But as the boys' sharpening senses found no evidence of danger, and as they saw Shriker's shadow on the blinds—drawn, tonight—courage hardened in them. Buddy was sure there was no shotgun trap, or, if there were, it operated only if the gate were opened. That Little Pie could climb the gate and return safely also seemed certain. What seemed less of a cinch was that he could exhume the body of Buzzer Atkins without being heard.

Little Pie whispered, "*Todo madre!*"

He rose to his feet an inch at a time. They stood together, watching Shriker's shadow on the blind as he carved off a chunk of steak and lifted it on his fork. Little Pie picked up the ladder and carried it to the gate. It was shorter than the gate was high, but he leaned it against the heavy hardware-cloth grille welded to the uprights. Buddy heard his teeth chattering. His breathing sounded uneven, like that of a boy circling just before a fight started. He was scared witless.

Then he crossed himself and started climbing.

Reaching the top of the gate, he found handholds between the dagger-like barbs welded to the top rail. He eased one foot into position atop the bar, then the other. Buddy prayed that a pants cuff was not snagged by one of those wicked spear points. Little Pie looked at the ground below, poised, then jumped. . . .

He made a perfect landing, and crouched. Shriker's shadow leaned forward as he shoveled some more food into his mouth. He took a swallow of coffee. Pulling the trowel from his shirt, Little Pie crawled to the lawn, rose, and walked slowly across it.

Buddy wanted to yell, "Go, *man*, go!" just as Little Pie used to root for him. The little guy had heart, like a fox standing off a dozen hounds. He reached the house, moved along to Buzzer's window, and sank from view into the deeper shadows.

Buddy could not hear the rasp of the trowel, but evidently Buzzer did, for there was a soft cat cry. Shriker straightened and looked around.

Fear locked Buddy up tight. *No—oh, no*! he whispered.

He heard Shriker say, "No use begging, you fat ol' thing! You've had your dinner. Can't have mine too."

Buddy sank to the ground, feeling blessed.

Suddenly he saw the ladder standing there. He was really playing like a rookie; for by now the ladder was supposed to have been slid under the gate for Little Pie's return trip.

He crawled out on the drive and with his fingers checked the narrow space beneath the gate. Huh! It was not very high. A stout iron rail half sunk in the ground carried the gate's wheels when it slid open. Fear brushed him with a sudden chill. What if there were not enough clearance to pass the ladder under the gate?

Carefully, he lowered the ladder to the ground. He raised one end and started to pass it under the gate. With a cold shudder, he realized it would not go.

Laying the ladder across the drive, he crawled back out of sight in the bushes. *Now what?* How come a picket fence had to be made of three-by-threes with inch-and-a-half slats? It could not pass between the spears, because of the hardware-cloth grille of the gate. The only way, he decided, was to heave the ladder over when Little Pie came back. Otherwise the crash of its landing would be heard.

His ears caught the scrape of metal in earth. *Easy, man*! he thought. Tilting back in his chair, Shriker seemed to listen for a moment, then resumed eating.

Buzzer whined again. There was another sound—like a small stick breaking. To Buddy's shock, the caretaker rose slowly and silently from his chair. He stood there a moment. Then, moving quietly, he paced toward the door. . . .

Buddy reared onto his knees and shouted.

"Take off!"

The floodlights came on like an explosion. In their brilliance he saw that Little Pie was already halfway across the lawn, chasing his shadow as it raced ahead of him. Under one arm he carried something like a rusty strongbox.

"The ladder!" he yelled. "*Amigo—!*"

The screen door burst open, and Shriker stepped out. As Little Pie reached the gate, Buddy called:

"I'll heave it to you. It wouldn't go under!"

But Little Pie was already scrambling up, risking impalement on the spear points. Shriker stood there like a giant. He saw Little Pie climbing, and must have assumed he was home safe—though he was miles from home—for abruptly he ducked back into the house.

There was a snarl of electric power in the shrubbery. Slowly the gate moved open. Little Pie bleated in fear, then realized what was happening. He dropped to the ground. The gate slid open. Little Pie raced through.

"Let's go!" he cried. He was off through the trees toward the thickets, where they would never be caught.

Buddy started to rise, but dropped back into the

bushes with a catch of his breath. Now *he* was the one who was trapped! For Shriker was coming like a sprinter, head working from side to side as he ran; or like a bone-crushing fullback going full bore. Buddy, who ran like a hound pup, knew he could never outdistance him.

He shrank back, hoping Shriker would not see him. Lying on the earth, two feet before him, was the ladder. His heart skipped. As the caretaker came through the gate with a rush, Buddy rocked the ladder up on its side.

Shriker hit it full speed. He went down without even stretching his hands out to break his fall. Landing flat, he skidded and came to a stop. He did not stir. The caretaker had taken the count.

Strange shadows dodged and raced around Shriker's body. Buddy thought, giddily, that he might be passing out. He was dizzy with excitement. Then he heard tires spinning in gravel. A car was coming—the shadows were those cast by its headlights. Running in a crouch, he streaked through the trees.

Before he reached the road, however, he saw Mrs. Podesta's station wagon rolling up the drive, and heard the baying of her carful of dogs.

21
Tomb of the Unknown Cat

For a while they heard each other's sounds in the brush, but did not call, each fearing the other might be a pursuer. Then Buddy called experimentally:

"K.I.!"

Little Pie's relieved voice replied softly, *"Todo madre!"*

In the crackling, sugary-scented dry brush, they squatted on the ground, panting.

"That was *so* close!" said Little Pie. He showed a quarter-inch with thumb and forefinger.

"You talk about close—did you see what happened to me?"

Little Pie had never looked back. Buddy told him about Shriker.

"He could be dead! We better work up an alibi fast."

"Would your folks back up a story?"

"Depends. If I told 'em the truth, maybeso. But I don't want them to have to go down to the station house and get worked over by those slobs. . . ."

"Gonna be questioned anyway. What we got to do is get down to your place and *stay put*. May be hours before they're after us. And we only got an extra hour or so to squeeze into our alibi—"

It sounded better, now that Buddy thought about it. Yet Shriker might have struck his head, or broken his neck, as he fell.

They trotted along dim animal trails in the brush. When these faded, there were child trails, leading them finally to Lopez Street. They whispered as they hustled past the small lamplit homes.

"Did you look in the box?" Buddy asked.

Little Pie shifted the box under his arm. "Not yet. But it stinks!"

"The cat! You got it."

"I got something that stinks is all I know."

Near Buddy's house they examined the box under a streetlight. Though dirty and pimpled with rust, the box did not look old. Its chrome latch was untarnished. Buddy had seen similar strongboxes, about the size of a fat dictionary, in the dime store for a dollar sixty-nine.

"Open it!" he urged.

"Not me! I'm going to put it in a paper carton and open it with a stick. Prob'ly full of maggots—"

Buddy's stomach bucked upward. They hurried on.

A quiet evening was in progress at the Williams home. Angie was doing her nails in the front room. Mrs. Williams was reading. Mr. Williams was going over a parolee's folder. From Ralphie's bedroom came the familiar strains of *Rudolph the Red-Nosed Reindeer* and the scrape of a spoon in a dish of dry Jell-O.

"This fellow McGoy—" Mr. Williams was saying. "I don't know whether he's snowing me or not. He's a salesman, and he says he's got to have a car or he can't work. But his parole agreement says no car. Now, if I ask for an exception—"

He glanced up. "Oh, hello, boys. How was the driving lesson?"

He said that, and then slowly, grimly, rose from the sofa.

"What's going on?" he demanded.

"Dad—" Buddy began.

Mr. Williams's face darkened. He started to walk toward Buddy. Then he said to his wife:

"You talk to them. I'll be in the kitchen. Call me when it's all over. I don't trust myself not to strike someone."

Angie laid down her emory board, sniffed and frowned. "What is that *horrible* smell?" she asked.

"That—that's Buzzer, we think," said Little Pie.

"*Buzzer!*" she shrieked. "Did somebody kill him?"

Little Pie placed the green box on a newspaper lying on the coffee table. Then, with the gravity of a mortician, he folded the paper across the strongbox. "We'll look later," he said.

Buddy started talking.

". . . So I guess," he said, finally, "they may come here again. If Shriker isn't dead—"

"Don't say it!" his mother said sharply. "Lloyd!"

Mr. Williams came in promptly. His face showed

that, despite his good intentions, he had been listening. Tightening his lips across his teeth, he said:

"I admire your intentions, boys, but I despise your judgment. Why didn't you tell me about the problem?"

"What could you do that we couldn't?"

"I have parolees," said Mr. Williams "who could go over, under, or through that fence in broad daylight. I have parolees who could steal a coffin from Executive Rest Suite at Meadow Glade Cemetery and look like workmen. In fact, one of them did, for the silver fittings. The point is, never assume a man like your father is a fool just because he's married and has a family—no harm meant, Lois," he told Mrs. Williams.

"You couldn't have asked one of your old boys to break the law, could you?" his wife said.

"I'd have thought of something better than this," said Mr. Williams. "Well, kids, what's your story? What do you plan to tell the police when they come?"

Buddy pulled open a drawer in a table where the playing cards were kept. He sat on the floor and started shuffling. "The truth," he said— "Sit down, Pie—The truth is, we played cards here this evening. . . ."

Little Pie dropped to the floor, and Angie hurriedly laid aside her nail things and joined them.

"After we left the Hannibals'," Buddy continued, "we walked by Crabby Mike's and had a pizza. Then we—"

A car whisked through the dry leaves of the street, slowed, stopped. Another car stopped. Mr. Williams strolled out on the porch. In a moment he returned. Placing his hands on his hips, he gazed at them.

"It's that lawyer woman and the police," he said. "Since they're the real lawbreakers, I'll do my best to back you up. You realize, of course, that if they break our story, I'll be charged, too. But you're my boy, and it seems to be something I've got to do for you. The last, probably."

Buddy's heart thumped.

From a mile away, you knew it was a cop's walk: *Clomp, clomp, clomp.* Absolute assurance—like if he walked headfirst into a door, it would automatically open with a murmur of greeting. *Clomp, clomp, clomp.* Heavy police leather climbed the steps from the street. *Clack, clack, clack*—high heels pierced the heavier sounds. Then the ugly tramp of many feet on the porch, and two raps at the door.

"Police," a man said.

Mr. Williams went to the door. "Good evening," he said.

Buddy twisted his neck to see. It was the young Mexican juvenile officer, Sergeant Sanchez, from Eighty-seventh Street. Behind him was the face of Mrs. Podesta. Mrs. Podesta cried:

"We've taken all we can! We're out of our minds with all this harassment—bows and arrows, ladders, digging up the shrubbery—"

The sergeant waved her to silence.

"Mr. Shriker claims your son and another boy trespassed on his property. He also says he was attacked. Assault with a deadly weapon, a felony."

Mrs. Podesta crowded forward, opened the door, and

slipped into the room. In her hands was a yellow legal pad. She began reading from it, " '. . . That on this day the aforementioned did feloniously and with intent to steal a strongbox of valuables buried on Mr. Shriker's premises. And that they did permit his beloved cat to escape for the second time. That—' "

" 'Beloved cat'!" Buddy snorted. "It was as dead as—"

Everyone stared at him. It was out. At once he felt better. He could not let his father lie for him and maybe go to jail too. His father had his problems, and he didn't ask Buddy's help with them. This one happened to be Buddy's.

Mr. Williams stared at him in sorrow. Other people were entering the room—stout Sergeant Swann, and Shriker. One side of the caretaker's face was skinned and his eye was swollen shut.

Mrs. Podesta saw the strongbox, suddenly, and almost dived at it. But Buddy had it first and jammed it under the sofa.

"Give me that!" she said. And to Sergeant Sanchez: "That's stolen property! I claim it for Mr. Shriker—"

Buddy asked his father. "Don't they need a search warrant to come in here?"

Sergeant Sanchez, removing his hat, now, said: "That's right, son. But I thought maybe you'd like to make a statement and clear things up."

"Since Mr. Shriker has an attorney," said Mr. Williams, "I think my son should have one, too. Of course, if Mrs. Podesta and he want to waive formalities and discuss matters—I'm sure no harm was intended, and the boys were only playing detective, you might say."

Sergeant Swann, red and puffing from the climb, dabbed at his brow with a handkerchief. His hair was gray and neatly waved, and he took pains not to disturb it.

"Why don't we," he suggested, "all sit down and talk it out? If nobody's got anything to hide, there's no reason to haggle around."

Buddy's mind raced to figure the odds. He was practically certain that they had the real Buzzer in the box. If that were true, and there was a false tooth in its head, things would look bad for Shriker. Also, if the stand-in cat was loose again, maybe Angie could catch him once more; and, with the pictures—

He decided he had nothing to lose.

"Okay by me," he said.

Mrs. Podesta's cold, fierce face beamed. She gave the tiniest flick of a glance at the tomb of the unknown cat.

"I'm sure Mr. Shriker has nothing to hide," she said. "Let's stop haggling and let the boys tell their story."

22
Buzzer Atkins Returns

No one knew Ralphie was listening until, when the pictures were produced for comparison by the police, he wailed from the doorway:

"That is doof God! That is bad!"

"Mom—" Buddy said, in agonized appeal.

Mrs. Williams, drawn and tired-looking, led Ralphie, weeping, off to his room.

Buddy exhibited the pictures. The Mexican sergeant compared them.

"Looks like the same cat, doesn't it, Swanny?"

"Sure does," said the other officer. "Ears are just exactly the same. One black, one white. How about that?"

"But the cat Shriker's got now has the ears backward!" Little Pie blurted. "We caught it, and we saw it."

"Absolutely false," murmured Mrs. Podesta reverently, as if it were a response to the Golden Text in a church service.

"Anyway," Buddy said, "it doesn't matter what kind of live cat he's got, if there's a dead one exactly like the one in that picture in this box, does it? It proves the real one's dead, right?"

"It would look mighty suspicious," agreed Sergeant Sanchez.

Mrs. Podesta smiled at Shriker. "You agree, don't you, Joel?" she said.

Shriker, holding a bloody handkerchief to his cheek, said: "Yes, ma'am. That's my strongbox, all right. I had some old coins in it, that's all. I don't know what the kids may have put in it to fun me—"

A wave of cold went down Buddy's chest. They were too sure of themselves! There was something funny about that box!

Sighing, Sergeant Swann dragged it onto the carpet. He laid the newspaper flat and placed the box on it. He sniffed, and made a face. Then he flipped up the latch. Before opening it, he looked at them all in hurt.

"A police officer's life ain't all peaches and cream," he said. "Don't you ever think it is."

Averting his face, he raised the lid. They crawled forward to look into the box . . .

A dead and moldy cat lay inside it. It was a black-and-white cat, a lean cadaver shedding hair and skin. A mess. But there was something wrong with this cat, aside from the fact that it was dead.

It had no head.

"Some mean kid," said Shriker thickly, "dug up my box and put an old dead cat in it! Ain't that a nice thing to do?"

Closing the box quickly, the policeman shoved it at him.

"No thanks. —No thank you!" said Shriker.

Sergeant Swann put the box on the porch.

Buddy sank onto the couch. Little Pie, still seated on the floor, scraped paint spots off his tennis shoes. A black fog enclosed Buddy.

If she wasn't already his lawyer, he thought, *I'd get her to defend me. Because she's got to be the smartest lawyer in the world.*

Mrs. Podesta, shaking her head slowly, said: "There are all kinds of charges we could make, but I'm going to make a suggestion to Mr. Shriker. That he waive charges if Mr. Williams agrees to a peace bond on his son, the same to be agreed to by the other parents involved. They will each put up a five-hundred-dollar bond, guaranteeing that their boys will stay strictly away from Hilltop Drive."

Mr. Williams hedged. "That would be pretty expensive."

Sergeant Swann picked up the photo of Buzzer and the arrow. "You know," he chuckled, "that was kind of clever, at that, the way those kids took this picture!"

A small figure rushed from the hallway into the room. It was Ralphie, in pajamas. Mrs. Williams was right after him. He snatched the picture from the policeman's hands.

"I don't like that! That is bad."

Swann looked more startled than angry. "What's wrong with it, son?" he asked.

"That is doof God deena tack!" wailed Ralphie. He threw the picture on the floor.

Puffing, Sergeant Swann bent to retrieve it. He squinted at the picture. Mrs. Podesta reached for it, but he gave her a quick cop stare and she turned away. Peering closely at the picture, the sergeant suddenly smiled.

"Oh, I see! They've printed the words on that sack of cat food backward, haven't they? Say, you've got sharp eyes, young fellow!"

He handed the picture to the other policeman. "Look at this, Sanchez—how stupid can a manufacturer get? The company that makes this cat food printed the words backward on it!"

In Buddy's head, a skyrocket fizzed, then took off with a roar and bursting lights. Joy was the smoke it left. In Sergeant Sanchez's face, he saw the same realization that had just come to him.

Rich, in printing the picture, had placed the negative upside down in the enlarger. So everything in the picture had been reversed!

Mrs. Podesta snatched at the picture, but Sanchez, giving her a cold stare, held it out of her reach. Shriker started to leave the house.

"Don't nobody leave the room!" said Sergeant Swann, beginning to sense, too, that he had missed something. The caretaker stood with bowed head by the door.

"It was your idea," he muttered to Mrs. Podesta.

"Shut up," the woman rapped.

To Ralphie, still wailing, Sergeant Sanchez said cheerfully:

"Look here, son—we're going to fix those words you don't like. You don't like things to read backward, do you—boy with good eyesight like yours? Look what happens when I hold it against the light!"

Sergeant Sanchez turned the shade of a reading lamp up like a spotlight. Then he placed the eight-by-ten print over it so that the light shone through. Now everything was reversed. The arrow slanted in from the other side. And Buzzer's black right ear was now white! The words on the sack were:

Cat and Dog Food.

Slowly, the sergeant read what was printed on the sack. "Pretty cute!" he said. "The boy reads like my kid in school. Phonics, don't they call it? You can read phonics just as good backward as forward."

Jumping up and down for joy, Ralphie saw that the phrase that had bothered him, because of some rigid sense of order in his brain, did make sense after all. "Cat and Dog Food!" he cried. "Buddy, Buddy, it is Cat and Dog Food!"

". . . I didn't want no part of it," Shriker was mumbling. "But you said you'd handle everything, get a cat just like the old one. Said this damn vet could find one for us—"

"Take the Fifth, Joel!" Mrs. Podesta hissed. "Will you *please* shut your—"

Big as he was, she had him out the door and halfway down the steps before the police could stop her.

For hours, Mr. Williams talked about false arrest and a lawsuit. He would certainly look into it. And Mr. Hannibal, when they telephoned him, said he would get going in the morning. The plans he had! First thing would be to organize teams to clean up the debris of the old club. Then get an architect to work on the plans he'd been fooling around with for years.

The excitement was over, but for hours they kept it inflated, as one might pump up a bicycle tire, by rehashing all the old stories about Shriker shooting at them; and what happened to the cat's head? and Rich pulling the biggest bobble in history by printing the picture with the negative upside down!

But finally the tire went flat, and Little Pie drifted home, yawning, and Ralphie fell asleep on the couch murmuring, "Cat and Dog Food," and Buddy said:

"Man, I'm beat," and went to bed.

Go, man, go! Little Pie used to yell at him from the poolside. And he had *gone, man, gone!* until his arms and legs tingled with exhaustion, and when he closed his eyes he felt unpleasantly as though he were being tipped over backward in a barber chair; or like falling from a high tower into a dark pool where shadows glided. . . .

Vaguely he heard his father pulling the chairs under the eaves of the porch, out of the night's dew. Last act before closing the store. Then he heard his voice, gently, as if speaking to a small child.

"Well, hello! Who are you? You're a friendly one, aren't you?"

There was a soft *meeow*!

From Angie's room, a cry of excitement. "Daddy! what is it?"

"I don't know, hon. Somebody's cat. Looks like the one in that picture the boys took—"

Buddy turned over and punched the pillow, grinning, and let himself slide into the pool called Sleep. Buzzer Atkins had come home.